At the sound of steps, Lark paused and stood aside. Two men came through the door. Lark was reaching for the knob of the screen they had let slam in his face when the taller man whirled on a boot heel. He said, "Hold it, mister. I want to talk to you. What are you doing in Acheron?"

Lark's eyebrows went up. "My business, chum."

"Don't get smart with me, pilgrim," the man said. "When I ask you a question, you answer." A big hand reached out and grasped Lark's shoulder.

Swiftly, smoothly, Lark pulled it from his shoulder and shoved it away. "A man could get hurt being so familiar," he said calmly.

"You sumbitch, I do as I please," the tall man said, and this time his grasp was cruel.

Like the strike of a snake, Lark's hands caught the thick wrist, levering the man's bulk over his shoulder. The man slammed to the boards, bounced and went skidding to the end of the porch. He rolled down the steps to the sidewalk. He sat there clutching an arm that hung limply, his face twisted in agony. Lark watched, cold-eyed.

As the man struggled to his feet, he looked at Lark with hate in his eyes. "I'll be seeing you, mister. Enjoy the next few days—they're all you've got. . . ."

# TALES OF THE OLD WEST

**SPIRIT WARRIOR**           (1795, $2.50)
by G. Clifton Wisler
The only settler to survive the savage indian attack was a little boy. Although raised as a red man, every man was his enemy when the two worlds clashed—but he vowed no man would be his equal.

**IRON HEART**           (1736, $2.25)
by Walt Denver
Orphaned by an indian raid, Ben vowed he'd never rest until he'd brought death to the Arapahoes. And it wasn't long before they came to fear the rider of vengeance they called . . . Iron Heart.

**WEST OF THE CIMARRON**           (1681, $2.50)
by G. Clifton Wisler
Eric didn't have a chance revenging his father's death against the Dunstan gang until a stranger with a fast draw and a dark past arrived from West of the Cimarron.

**HIGH LINE RIDER**           (1615, $2.50)
by William A. Lucky
In Guffey Creek, you either lived by the rules made by Judge Breen and his hired guns—or you didn't live at all. So when Holly took sides against the Judge, it looked like there would be just one more body for the buzzards. But this time they were wrong.

**GUNSIGHT LODE**           (1497, $2.25)
by Virgil Hart
When Ned Coffee cornered Glass and Corey in a mine shaft, the last thing Glass expected was for the kid to make a play for the gold. And in a blazing three-way shootout, both Corey and Coffee would discover how lightening quick Glass was with a gun.

# THE DEVIL'S BAND

## BY ROBERT McCAIG

ZEBRA BOOKS

KENSINGTON PUBLISHING CORP.

ZEBRA BOOKS

are published by

KENSINGTON PUBLISHING CORP.
21 East 40th Street
New York, N.Y. 10016

SECOND PRINTING SEPTEMBER 1986

Printed in the United States of America

*"Ill fares the land, to hastening ills the prey*
*Where wealth accumulates and men decay."*

. . . The Deserted Village
Oliver Goldsmith (1725–1774)

# Chapter I

She's not much different from a hundred other towns I've passed through on these western prairies, Lark thought. Just as hot, just as dusty, just as weather-worn and warped. Name's a little different, though—the depot sign reads ACHERON. Likely some remittance man had his wry joke, flaunting his aborted Oxford education by suggesting this synonym for HELL. The guy didn't miss the mark far at that, today anyhow, with the burg baking in sunlight like molten brass, and sweating in a gritty breeze hot enough to curl a she-wolf's hair. The only place that looks cool is the top of that sawtooth of snow-capped peaks to the west—thirty miles away? Fifty? A hundred? Who can tell through these dancing heat waves?

The bell of the locomotive began to clang tentatively. Lark picked up his valise and crossed the cinder platform. Time enough later when he was settled to send a drayman for his steamer trunk. Lark was aware of the curious glances of the handful of men gathered for the daily ritual of meeting the westbound. None of the men spoke to him. He crossed the dusty side street and was striding down the main drag by the time the engine hooted and chuffed westward in a spatter of hot cinders.

Lark's boot heels echoed hollowly on the plank sidewalk. The main street was almost empty, the only life an occasional pedestrian or a creaky wagon. At the hitchrails in front of the saloons a few cowponies stood patient in the heat, a flicking of tails or a shuddering of hides their defense against the flies.

One of the few two-story buildings among the false fronts of Main Street bore the faded sign HOTEL. Its porch chairs were empty of the usual loafers, those ancient observers who spend so many of their vacant hours sitting that they seem as permanent fixtures as the porch posts. Lark shifted his valise from right hand to left and went up the three steps toward the screen door.

At a thud of steps from inside Lark paused and stood aside. Two men came through the screen door. As he passed Lark, the taller man's glance slid across his face like a sweep of brush over stencil. The two were past and Lark was reaching for the knob of the screen they had let slam in his face when the taller man whirled on a boot heel. He said "Hold it, mister. I want to talk to you." His voice grated, flint on steel.

Hand on the knob, Lark said, "Your openers."

"What the hell are you doing in Acheron?" the man asked.

Lark's eyebrows went up. "My business, chum.

8

Not yours."

"Don't get smart with me, pilgrim," the man said. "When I ask you a question, you answer." A big hand reached out and grasped Lark's shoulder, clamping hard.

Swiftly, smoothly, Lark's right hand caught the man's wrist, pulled the hand from his shoulder and shoved it away. "A man could get hurt being so familiar," he said calmly.

"You sumbitch, I do as I please," the tall man said, and this time his grasp was cruel, fingers digging into the flesh of Lark's shoulder. "Now answer me, just who the hell—"

Like the strike of a snake, Lark's hands caught the thick wrist. He turned toward the street, levering the man's bulk over his shoulder. The man slammed to the boards, bounced and went skidding to the edge of the porch. He rolled down the steps to the sidewalk. He sat there dazed, moaning, clutching an arm that hung limply. His face was twisted in agony. Lark watched, cold-eyed. The hand of the stocky companion dropped toward his holstered six-gun.

"I wouldn't, pal," Lark said curtly. "You pull that iron on me and I'll take it away and make you eat it." At the command in Lark's voice the hand stopped, the thumb ostentatiously hooked into the gun belt. The man's round face went as blank as a schoolboy's caught in a melon patch.

The tall man struggled to his feet, still holding his arm. He groaned, "C'mon, Badeye. I think this bastard busted my shoulder. I gotta get to Doc Kermit. Gimme a hand here."

Badeye stared at Lark with eccentric eyes, turned and went down the steps to help his companion. Lark stood solidly braced, staring at the two. His right hand played with the left lapel of his jacket. He said nothing.

As the tall man leaned on Badeye, he looked at Lark with hate in his eyes. And hate was in his voice as he said, "I'll be seeing you, mister. Enjoy your next few days, they're all you've got. Men who cross the Joshuans don't live long afterward."

Lark didn't answer. Though the tall man's malevolence was like a smoldering fire, Lark had dealt with hardcases as mean, or meaner. Disgust welled up in Lark, not fear. Still, plain common sense kept him facing the street until the two men, one supporting the other, reached the next street corner. Only then did he pick up his valise and open the screen door.

The hotel lobby was scarred and dusty, dim, for its cracked green blinds were pulled against the heat. It smelled of sweat and stale beer and old tobacco. From over the desk a motheaten buffalo head leered at Lark with dull glassy eyes. From beyond a partition came the muted sound of voices. When no one came to the desk, Lark pinged the hand bell, once and again.

Slow footsteps sounded. The man who shuffled through the door behind the desk was past middle age, with a lined acid face, a white mustache stained with tobacco juice. His face was wry with distaste or annoyance as he stared at Lark. With an automatic gesture he adjusted black sateen sleeve protectors.

A vinegar puss, Lark thought. For sheer orneriness, Lark did not speak.

The hotel man lost the silent duel. Grumpily he asked, "You want somethin'?"

"A room," Lark said.

"Dollar a night, cash in advance."

"Is that with or without bedbugs?"

Lark had touched a nerve. The man said angrily, "By God, mister, we run a clean place! You ast anybody if Shank Morris don't have the sheets changed onst a week. Lissen, you find a bug, just lemme know, and I'll—I'll make it right. I got my pride, mister."

"Good for you," Lark said. He spun a gold eagle across the counter. "When I've used that up, tell me, and I'll give you another like it."

Somewhat mollified, Shank Morris reversed the register and shoved it toward Lark. "Gonna stay a spell, Mr.—Mr. Lark?" he asked, as Lark penned *Justin P. Lark, Denver, Colorado,* and put the pen back in its raw potato. Lark saw that the page was headed THE MORRIS HOUSE, ACHERON, M.T., and dated correctly—*JULY 8, 1889.* Names ran three-quarters of the length of the page. He scanned them, but saw none that aroused his interest.

"Be staying a week, two weeks, who knows?" he said. "Depends on how long my business takes."

"And your business is . . . ?"

"Is my business," Lark said blandly. "A pretty tough town you have here, Shank Morris."

The clerk turned back from the keyboard behind him with the key he had selected. "Number twenty-

11

two, Mr. Lark. Best room I have in the house. Whadda you mean, tough?"

"A couple of rannies came out of your hotel just as I came in," Lark said. "Both of 'em wearing guns. Sheriffs in most cowtowns enforce rules about packing iron in the city limits."

"They got a rule here, all right, but—what did them men look like?"

Lark reached out and took the key on its brass tab. Morris's air of innocence did not deceive him. It was an axiom that the desk clerk knew everything that went on in his hotel to the last detail. The two men had been in the hotel. He said "One tall, mean face, spikey mustache. The other, square like an outhouse, wrinkled face, one cocked eye. The tall one said something sounded like 'the Joshuans.'"

Morris's head snapped up, concern on his face. "Blackie Legrand and Badeye Klaus. You didn't tangle with 'em, for God's sake?"

"Afraid I did," Lark said. "The tall guy got sudden with me and tried to savage me. I threw him out in the street. Dislocated his shoulder. Last I saw of 'em they were on their way to find a doctor."

Morris licked lips suddenly gone dry. He cleared his throat, made a false start, and blurted out, "Gosh, Mr. Lark, I just remembered, got a party comin' in on the eastbound I promised rooms and they're the last I have. Afraid you'll hafta look elsewhere for a bed." He reached his hand out for the key.

Lark dropped the key into his pocket. "Now,

old-timer, you don't lie worth a damn. I'm rooming in your hostelry whether you like it or not. What's about Legrand and Klaus and the Joshuans that puts the yellow up your neck?"

Morris's glance darted right and left. He leaned across the desk, and said in a hoarse whisper, "Around here we don't talk about the Joshuans, Mr. Lark. Leastwise where anybody can hear. All I'll say is to warn you if you've crossed 'em, you're a dead man. So I don't want you killed here, bloodyin' up my hotel."

"I'll take pains to see that doesn't happen," Lark said calmly. "It would help if you gave me the lowdown, Shank."

The clerk shook his head stubbornly. "I ain't about to say nothin'. It's too risky. You'll find out soon enough, God help you."

Lark stood a silver dollar on edge on the counter and held it upright with his left index finger. With his right forefinger he stroked it once, twice, then caught the edge of the coin with his hidden thumb. The coin spun in a blur toward Morris. The man caught it, slipped it into a vest pocket and stood waiting.

"In appreciation of future services," Lark explained. "There will be more of those, if—but never mind for now. Morris, have the drayman pick up my trunk at the depot and bring it here. Put the charge on my bill. Where's the best place to eat?"

"We don't have no dining room here at the hotel—too much trouble tryin' to keep a sober cook. Your best bet is the Chinaman's couple blocks down the street. Or the Maverick, though the boys call that Ptomaine Joe's."

"Guess I'll give the Chinaman a whirl. And if any hardcases packing six-guns come looking for me, stall 'em." He picked up his valise and started for the stairs.

"T'aint funny, Mr. Lark. You'll see," Morris retorted ominously.

Lark chuckled and went on up the stairs.

He found Room 22 surprisingly light and clean for a Montana cowtown hotel. The bedding looked decent, the carpet was faded but clean. Curtains of dotted swiss ruffled at the open window in the faintest of breezes. Lark hung his jacket in the wardrobe. He unbuckled his shoulder holster and dropped the snub-nosed .38 on the dresser. Doffing his soiled, sweaty shirt, he poured water from the pitcher into the big china basin. He scrubbed hands and face and scarred torso and dried on a clean towel. The tiny draft of air from the open window felt pleasantly cool on his damp skin.

Shirtless, he opened his valise and packed the things from it into the dresser drawers. He hung a clean shirt on the back of a chair. Combing his hair, in the cloudy mirror he saw without pleasure that his hairline was receding further, and there were more patches of gray at his temples. Then he shrugged. A wonder my hair isn't snow-white, he thought, after some of the cases I've been on. Like that affair at Stoneman's Gap a few years ago— that was a humdinger. Though if need be I'd tackle the Redtops again singlehanded, for it was

Stoneman's Gap that brought me Sonya.

He dropped into the creaky rocker. He reached for the tobacco and the Riz la Croix papers he had put on the table. He rolled a cigarette, one of the few he allowed himself each day. Lighting the quirly, he relaxed as the blue smoke drifted in slow spirals across the room.

After that dull and wearisome train ride today, tomorrow will be soon enough to tackle the agency's business, Lark thought. In an hour or so I'll wander down the drag. Maybe have a couple beers, then tackle the Chinese restaurant and see if it is as non-fatal as Morris implied. All the time keeping my ears open, of course. Like to know more about this Joshuans business. Whoever they are they've got the Indian sign on Shank Morris, for one. I'll keep an eye out for Legrand and Klaus, too. Oh well, I've crossed trails with curly wolves like those two before. I don't like 'em, but I can handle 'em.

Damn, I wish I wasn't stuck with this assignment! I'll admit Eames was up a tree, with Belote in Nevada on that U.P. deal, and Harnish staked out in Boulder buying high-grade. I'll give the boss credit, he didn't say I had to go, just asked if I would. So what could I say? The Pinkerton brass back in Chicago had named me assistant bureau chief with a fat raise, so I guess they had me over a barrel. So I said I'd come.

If I could have brought Sonya along, everything would have been jake. The two of us are a formidable team. But with the new baby—man, that kid does look like me, or so Sonya says. Hope he grows up to be a damned sight smarter than his old man and never goes to work for the Pinkerton's National Detective Agency. Bemused by his thoughts, Lark dropped into a doze.

Later, in clean shirt and bow tie, his jacket and trousers brushed and the dust carefully polished from his half-boots, Justin Lark left his room and went down the stairs. He paused a moment, head cocked, hearing low voices from a back room, and the unmistakable click and clatter of poker chips. Morris was not at the desk and the lobby was empty. Outside, Lark paused on the porch with his usual caution, then strode down the street in the slanting sunlight of late afternoon. The false fronts reached out long shadows across the dusty street, a touch of blessed coolness.

Of the half-dozen saloons, the Silver Dollar looked the least run-down, its sign less bullet-riddled, the gold leaf letters on its windows visible enough to prove the glass had been washed within recent memory. Lark pushed through the swinging doors and stopped a moment to adjust his vision to the dimness. Then he crossed to the long bar.

The saloon was not crowded. A few morose characters stood with a foot on the brass rail. Two desultory card games—pitch or euchre, Lark supposed—occupied two side tables. Lark ordered beer. He sipped the cold brew gratefully. He stood half turned, boot heel caught on the rail, elbow on the mahogany. He saw no inquiring glances. No one seemed interested in him, no one attempted conversation. Not even the bartender, who seemed soured on life, not liking his job or his customers as he scrubbed the surface of the bar eternally with a damp cloth.

No sign of Legrand or Klaus, or any other trouble, Lark decided. Legrand won't be in much shape for a go-round for a couple weeks, nor do I regret that. A dislocated shoulder is damn near as bad as a break, and hurts worse. Maybe that will teach the bastard not to threaten strangers. Serves him right.

Finishing his beer, Lark ordered another. As he drank, he saw no developments, hostile or friendly. He left the Silver Dollar and found the Chinese restaurant. He had an acceptable meal of beef pot roast, potatoes and gravy, and canned peach pie. He paid his fifty cents and left, toothpick in mouth. He debated having a drink, thought better of it, and went back to the Morris House.

There was a stout, graying woman behind the desk now, probably Mrs. Morris, Lark thought, for she looked at him with undisguised curiosity as he crossed the lobby. He held up his key and she nodded. Upstairs, he unlocked Room 22. He stood in the doorway a moment, making sure his two subtle indicators had not been disturbed. They had not, so he locked the door behind him.

The long Montana twilight was darkening now. Lark lit the oil lamp and placed it in the sconce on the wall. He shucked off his boots and wriggled his toes in satisfaction. Before he dropped into the rocker, he made sure it was out of direct line with the buildings across the street. A good hand with a Sharp's. . . .

As he rolled a cigarette, it came to him with something of a shock that Mrs. Shank Morris, if it were indeed she, was only the second woman he had seen in Acheron. The other had been the silent Chinese waitress in the restaurant. Lark filed away this discrepancy for what it was worth in the mental picture he was building of this town.

At this hour most cowtowns would be coming to life, the orchestrions in the saloons planging away, noisy greetings along the street, shouts and loud laughter. Not in Acheron. He had sensed a gloomy, suspicious mood in the saloon, in the restaurant, in this hotel. The mood did not lighten. The town remained stolid and wary. I'll get little help locally on my case, Lark thought. The people, by God, are scared spitless.

He sat quiet a long time as the twilight deepened into dusk and the dusk into night. Still Acheron sprawled torpid, with, occasionally, the sound of horses, of boots thumping on the board sidewalk, or a voice raised and quickly stilled. A strange town, Lark thought, and decided to go to bed.

He was unbuttoning his shirt when he heard the swift echo of footsteps in the hall outside his room. There was a sharp knock on his door panel. He picked up the Colt .38 Lightning from the dresser, stuck it in his belt and went to the door. He called, "Who is it?"

"An old friend, Justin. Let me in," came a woman's voice.

Turning the key, he opened the door a foot, two.

Arms went around his neck, a soft feminine body pressed against him. A throaty voice cried, "So sorry I'm late, darling." Then she whispered close to his ear, "Let me inside, quickly, for God's sake."

Lark swung the girl into the room, holding her with a strong arm. With his free hand he slammed and locked the door. Pushing the girl against the wall, he ran hands under her kimono down her body and between her thighs. He was startled to find that the slim body was naked under the ruffled kimono. Releasing her, he stepped back.

"You didn't have to do that!" she cried angrily. She pulled her robe tighter around her and knotted the belt.

"A deringer doesn't take much space, lady. Now, what's this all about? How did you know my name?"

The crimson of embarrassment was fading from her face. He saw that she was pretty, even beautiful, in the light of the oil lamp. Reaching up, he turned up the wick and the lamp brightened. Waiting for her answer, he gave her a frank survey.

"I—I'm not that kind of woman, like—I mean—" she said.

"You're not a whore? Then why did you act like one?" he asked tersely. "I want the truth, young lady, or out you go."

Her lips were a taut line of anger. "Because I had to see you, and there's a nasty little man who has the room next to mine. He watches every move I make. So I thought I'd mislead him by pretending to be—uh, what you said."

"How do I know you are not?"

"Because, Mr. Justin Lark, I'm your client, Diane Carvell."

## Chapter II

Lark stared at the girl, nonplussed. Warily he asked, "You are? You seem to know who I am, but how and why?"

Her dark eyes were puzzled. "You are Justin Lark, from Pinkerton's Denver office, aren't you?" She fumbled in the pocket of her robe. "Here is the telegram I had from Mr. Eames yesterday."

The message on the yellow sheet read:

> DENVER COLO.
> JULY 7 1889
>
> D. CARPENTER
> ACHERON M.T.
> OUR ENGINEER JUSTIN LARK WILL MEET YOU IN ACHERON TOMORROW OR FOLLOWING DAY STOP MAN IS QUITE COMPETENT AND TRUSTWORTHY TO MAKE SURVEY YOU REQUESTED
>
> S W EAMES
> CHIEF ENGINEER

Lark folded the telegram and tore it across and again. He dropped the scraps in an ash tray and touched a match to them. When the paper was consumed he crushed the ashes into powder.

"Since your business is so touchy you and Sam Eames have to use code, we'd better not leave any evidence lying around," he said. "You say your real name is Carvell?"

"Yes. But Mr. Eames told me to use the name Diane Carpenter here."

Lark reached over and took the girl's long-fingered hand. He said, "Hello, Miss Diane. No hard feelings over my suspicions? I've been here only half a day but this town already has me jumpy."

"Wait until you've been here two days as I have. There's something about the town, and the people that is—well, uncomfortable. But for now, Mr. Lark—Justin—no, no hard feelings. Apparently Mr. Eames did not brief you on my case."

"He didn't have a chance," Lark said. "I got back from an investigation in Colorado Springs to find orders from Sam to get here to Acheron as fast as I could. Sam had to rush to Boulder where a highgrading case had boiled over. His scribbled note said I would meet a client here, but I did not suspect it would be a very pretty young woman."

There was a coolness in her voice as she said, "Remember, Justin, our relationship is merely that of detective and client. Nothing more."

"You haven't any worries on that score, Diane," Lark said, with a chuckle. "When I went home in Denver to pack my keister, my wife Sonya had it all

22

ready. She's a Pinkerton op too, or was until the baby came. She's on leave of absence right now. So I kissed her and the baby good-bye and caught the train, to count the days until I get back to them.''

"So you're a family man. Good. I hope you don't have cause to regret handling my case, Justin. It may prove extremely dangerous.''

"All in the day's work, for which Pinkerton's pays me an excellent salary, though they make me earn it. Of course in the long run the client must pay for it all, plus a healthy percentage.''

Diane Carvell smiled, showing quick perception. "Don't worry about costs, Justin. I am quite wealthy, and I'm prepared to spend every cent I own to bring my family back to me.''

Lark recognized the girl's sincerity. He spun the straight chair around and straddled it, arms on the back, and faced her in the rocker. He said, "Let's begin at the beginning, then, young lady. Give me chapter and verse of the problem. But keep your voice low, the walls of these jerry-built cracker boxes are all-fired thin.''

"It's a strange story, Justin, even weird,'' the girl said. "To begin with—well, there's my family background. You've heard of Christy Carvell, the mining promoter. Christy was my father.''

"Of course. He developed the Winking Jack mine in Leadville.''

"And the Cormorant at Central City,'' she said. "But when he sold out daddy didn't sink his money back into holes in the ground, like some of the others. He moved to Denver, built our big mansion, and put his fortune into real estate and

23

railroads. My mother had died when I was quite young, but daddy lived until three years ago. When he died I became the head of the family."

"And your family is—?"

"Not even uncles and aunts, just my brother Lavon, nineteen, and my twenty-one-year-old twin sisters Kristin and Gracia, plus myself, an aging spinster of twenty-six."

"Spinster by your own choice, I'm sure," Lark said gallantly.

She smiled. "Perhaps. Now note the ages, Justin, you'll see why they are important. When daddy died I had just come home from college with my degree from the Colorado School of Mines at Golden."

"Good Lord! You're a mining engineer?"

"I am indeed—I've even worked at it for a short time. I found good use for my knowledge in settling daddy's estate. Finances were no problem, but daddy had spoiled Lavon and the twins rotten, they were handed everything on a silver platter. The girls are beauties, intelligent, glowing with health. They considered the world their oyster, and it was."

"Your case concerns them? I'd like to meet them."

"I pray that you will, Justin. Then there's Lavon, a different type, thoughtful, moody, good at what interests him, terrible at what doesn't. When the family responsibilities fell upon me, I began to encounter resistance to the authority I had neither asked for nor wanted to use. My darling trio wanted things their way, and only their way, though they leaned on me."

"I suppose you became nurse, mentor, confessor, and rescuer from trouble."

"I think lion tamer best describes my role. But I did manage to hold the family together without disaster until six months ago. Then the twins turned twenty-one."

"And could defy your authority as they pleased?"

"Yes. But Justin, though they were legally adults, how could I abandon the darling idiots? Somebody had to watch out for two beautiful, mercurial girls who had each, without let or hindrance, sole control of one million dollars."

Lark gasped. "Did you say a million?"

"I did. The expression is 'a cool million' but in the hands of the twins it was burning hot. Daddy had set up a trust fund for each of us, reverting to us on our twenty-first birthday. Mine gave me two summers of study in Europe, a working ranch near Fort Collins, and some investments. But those heavenly twins . . ." She shook her head.

"They didn't fall in with shady characters?" Lark asked.

"Not exactly. Really, our troubles began with my young brother Lavon. The boy is a student with a brilliant, inquisitive mind. He takes great interest in new ideas, though he may not stick with them. One day Lavon is a philosopher, the next a budding parson. He has flitted from atheism to Buddhism, his mentors range from Robert Ingersoll to St. Francis of Assisi. He's like a weathervane swinging in every theological wind. He could hardly endure waiting for his trust fund, because he wanted to devote every cent of it to feeding the poor of the world. A laudable ambition, but I was glad his million was tied up until the boy had better judgment."

"Evidently a young man of good heart," Lark murmured.

"Too aimlessly good," Diane Carvell said, frowning. "As a result of his whims you and I are in Acheron. You see, Justin, a man came to Denver—a strange man in his middle years, muscular, a great brindle beard and hair like an Old Testament prophet. Dynamic, with piercing eyes, and a mellow, musical voice. I never met the man, but I saw him once. He is the leader of a sect in the Montana Rockies called 'the New Eden.' His apostles or acolytes refer to him as *The Shepherd*. His real name is Hiram Joshua Danville."

"What was his mission in Denver?"

"Recruiting. Gathering new blood and new money for his sect. The man has power, Justin, a mysticism allied, I think, to mesmerism. His theme was 'give up all temporal things and follow me. In our commune it is one for all and all for one.' He filled Lavon and some others with a holy hunger. I did my best to dissuade the boy, but he followed The Shepherd when Danville left the city."

"Maybe this is another passing whim," Lark said.

"Unfortunately, no," she said. "He wrote me, his letter signed Lavon Joshua Carvell. It was ecstatic—in the New Eden it is 'from each according to his ability, to each according to his needs.' He asked for money, and I sent him five hundred dollars. He wrote again, asking for more. But the second letter, Justin, had snippets of words and whole sentences, scissored out."

"Censored? Diane, what of the others who left with The Shepherd?"

"None have returned, all have written home for money. I began to fear for my brother's sanity and his safety. I didn't like the way things were adding up. On checking, I found that all the people Danville had recruited, young, middle-aged, or old, came from wealthy families."

"You smelled a bunco racket. And so do I," Lark said.

"That was only the beginning. Last month our twins disappeared, with them their suitcases, clothes, jewelry. I was frantic until a frightened maid brought me a note they had left: 'High adventure lies beyond the sunset. We go there to seek sweet Eden. Romance beyond price awaits us where the sun stands still. Farewell, darling sister. We love you.'"

"They had followed Lavon. What did you do?" Lark asked.

"The Carvell bank accounts are important enough that I could wangle some information from the bank people. Kris and Gracia had drawn out fifty thousand dollars each. Certified checks to the order of Lavon Joshua Carvell. Since his true middle name is Christopher, I knew he had given the order. Those little snips had been in steady correspondence with him, it was evident. They

27

followed him, for they adored him. He has always been able to dominate them, though he was younger."

"So you went to Pinkerton's in Denver."

"Yes, after I had written Von at Acheron, M.T., where his letters had been postmarked. That letter came back stamped UNKNOWN, as did my letters to the sheriff and to Hiram Danville. I could see the danger in pushing the matter farther myself, so I dumped the whole mess into the lap of Mr. Eames."

"He sent you here with orders to lie low."

"Yes, until help from his office arrived. His few inquiries showed this New Eden thing was extensive, and possibly deadly. He told me to say I wanted to diversify my cattle operation by expanding to Montana, so was looking for good land to buy. I have learned one thing that might interest you—the hierarchy of New Eden, the men who run the spread are called *Joshuans*, and everyone in this unfriendly close-mouthed town is afraid of them."

"So that's who those two were," Lark said. "Diane, I tangled with a couple of hardcases who threatened me with the wrath of the Joshuans. Legrand and Klaus, the names were. They looked like killers who would scrag you at the drop of a Stetson. So we'd better walk very, *very* carefully."

"Yes. There's big money involved. Just think, Justin, a hundred thousand already just from the twins, and they are only two in many."

She stood up with a quick, lithe movement. She grasped the back of the rocker so tightly her

28

knuckles showed white. Her lovely face was taut with repressed panic. She said "Justin, I'm terrified. This mysterious affair that has engulfed Von and the girls—the money, the censored letter—what can we do? This land is savage; its people are hostile. Where are my dear ones in this cruel outland? And why, Justin, why?"

He put an arm around her shoulders, feeling the shaking of her slim body. "We'll get answers, kid," he assured her. "Just take it easy. It won't help to get hysterical. We'll get your family out safe and sound, I'll stake my reputation and the rep of the Pinkerton Agency on that."

Growing calmer, she sat down again. Brushing away a tear, she said, "We've got to, Justin. They are—they are all I have. Have you any plan in mind?"

"Not until I have more informtion. We must move slowly, Diane. We must find some source of information inside New Eden. Until we know the lay of the land, know who is with us and against us, we're pretty helpless."

She smiled shakily. "From what I've seen, the whole population of Acheron is against us. The people seem so surly and suspicious."

"That may turn to our advantage," Lark said. "If they are ruled by fear, fear creates opposition. There are ways . . . We should have another wire from Sam Eames with more information. And I'll work on Shank Morris, the owner of this hotel. I think he knows plenty. Diane, we'll have to have a couple saddle horses and saddles. I'm not about to ride this rough country in a buckboard."

"Nor I," the girl said. "Justin, I know horses. Daddy always had a fine stable. Suppose I look around tomorrow to find two good saddlers."

"That's great. In a couple of days we can start riding around the county, looking for a ranch you want to buy. And you'll be damned particular."

"And you'll be my ranch manager, advising me," she said.

"You've got it, Mrs. Carpenter ma'am. We'll figure out a good cover story that Eames can back up if there are any inquiries. Next, can you handle a gun?"

"I'm no great shucks with a pistol, but I can handle a rifle better than most. I've done my share of mountain hunting."

"Good. We'd better keep our shooting irons handy from now on. Listen, I'll walk you back to your room so you can get your beauty sleep. Not that you need it."

She took his arm as they went down the hall. "Oh, Justin, you say the nicest things!" she cried, simpering. "I'm so happy you are here to help me find my new ranch."

The door of the room next to hers was open a crack. Lark said loudly "I'm glad too, baby. Gives me a chance to spark the prettiest gal east of the Rockies." In front of the door, he swept Diane into his arms and kissed her warmly. "That'll give you something to dream on, chickie," he said.

"Oh, Justin, you're so masterful!" Diane cried. She went into her room and shut the door.

The crack of light at the door of the adjoining room disappeared as the door went softly shut.

Lark walked back to his own room, grinning. We gave the spy an earful, he thought. Hope he enjoyed it.

## Chapter III

Diane was dressed and ready when Lark rapped on the door of her room at seven o'clock. The girl looked pert and lovely in a dark blue tailored riding habit. Her full skirt proved to be one of the new divided skirts becoming popular in the West, though somewhat shocking to those who thought any woman riding astride was less than a lady. "If I'm buying horses, I've got to try them out," she explained.

"Most becoming," Lark said, and they went down the stairs.

Breakfast at the Chinese restaurant was quite palatable, laced with the sauce of hunger. As they ate, Lark said, "Buying horses, saddles and tack, plus a pair of rifles, will cost you a pretty penny."

"I'll consider it an investment," she said. "I wish I could have my own saddle from my ranch, but I'll have to make do."

"Your ranch at Fort Collins? You spend a lot of time there?"

"When I can, I love the place. Living my childhood in the mountains spoiled me for city dwelling. I have a good ranch foreman who looks after things. Ours isn't a big operation, but it's rewarding. For instance, we're carrying out some cattle breeding experiments, trying to get more beef per animal. Crosses and so on."

"What's the name of your place?"

"Rafter C. The former owners, the Carpenters, were Colorado pioneers. But the family petered out and they sold to me a few years ago."

"So that's why you gave *Carpenter* to Sam Eames for a cover name. You have a real identity if anyone asks."

Diane nodded. "And the *Mrs.* gives me a husband," she added, dimpling. "Just in case any man gets ideas."

Lark leaned closer. "Diane, I picked up a long night letter from Sam Eames this morning. From what he says, your *Mrs.* wouldn't slow up The Shepherd. Sam has picked up rumors of plural marriage at New Eden."

"Oh God, Justin, no!" Diane exclaimed. "Those beautiful young sisters of mine—he wouldn't dare!"

"I think Danville has the world by the tail and will dare anything," Lark said seriously. "We've got to swing into action soon, lady."

She bit her lip. "Couldn't we go to the governor?"

"Officialdom is our last resort," he said. "There's no telling which politicians Danville has on his payroll and in his pocket. We can be sure he has Hardup County sewed up."

Leaving, Lark paid the little Chinese girl,

adding a generous tip. For the first time the solemn Oriental child gave him a shy smile.

Lark and Diane walked down Main Street toward the bank. Diane was opening an account with a certified check for $5,000. She said, "That will make Acheron sit up and take notice."

"It will that. The news will be sizzling along the moccasin telegraph in half an hour," Lark said, smiling. "There's your man now."

Ahead a rotund man in black broadcloth and wing collar with striped cravat was hurrying to the bank door, a ring of keys in his hand. As the man held the door for Diane to enter, Lark said, "I'll meet you in the hotel lobby about noon. First one there waits for the other." She nodded, and he went on down the street.

He had located the office of the Acheron *Argus* the afternoon before. Now he found the door still locked, and no sign of activity through the dusty windows. He turned away and headed for the ugly brick building that blocked the far end of the street. He had learned that was the Hardup County courthouse, which housed the sheriff's office, jail, and other county services.

There was no great rush to begin work in Hardup County, Lark learned. There were no horses at the hitchrail, nor carriages in the wagon yard. He walked clear around the building, and frustrated, went back to the hotel.

Finding Shank Morris behind the desk, Lark performed his little trick with the spinning dollar. This time Morris was ready and the coin was swept away and into a pocket swiftly. "Mornin', Mr.

Lark. Sleep well?" the hotelman asked. Lark caught a hint of a leer.

That nasty little spy next to Diane's room, Lark decided. Just what we wanted. "Like a top, Shank," he said. "Say, I see you have a newspaper in your town."

"Yeah, what passes for one—Acheron *Argus*."

"Happen to have a recent copy?"

"Last week's. 'Nother one won't be out until Thursday. Got the paper around here somewhere. Yeah, here you are."

Lark retired to a creaky saloon chair across the lobby. He raised the curtain for light and began perusing the weekly. Just as Acheron was like a hundred other cowtowns, so was the *Argus* like other weeklies. A column of local comings and goings, ranch news, cattle markets (still down), a modicum of advertising, a couple pages of boilerplate. News stories on a fatal shooting at a sheep ranch (not important), and the wedding of a local bigwig (important). Not a word about the New Eden, or The Shepherd, nor the Joshuans.

Lark gave the paper back to Morris. "Shank," he asked, "what kind of guy is this Thomas T. Toney, the editor?"

"Well, he ain't no crusader, and that's for sure. Tom's not a bad guy when he's sober. When he's drinkin' he draws to inside straights and bobtail flushes and bluffs on a low pair. He knows dam' near everything that goes on in Hardup County, but he don't print it all. Wouldn't pay."

"Some things best unsaid if a man wants to stay healthy, eh? Say, Shank, Mrs. Carpenter wants me to check on some land ownerships. Who is the best one to see at the courthouse?"

"Kate Muldoon at the county assessor's office. Joshua Mordecai is the assessor, but he ain't there much. Don't know much, either. Kate, she's sharp. She'll give you what you need and a smile, too."

"Thanks, Shank, I'll see Miss Muldoon then," Lark said and turned away. He paused as Morris said with a kind of urgency "Remember, Mr. Lark, we was just shootin' the breeze. I didn't say nothin'."

"Of course not, Shank. You were just being neighborly," Lark said, and left.

Lark found the door of the *Argus* office open this time. A tall, lean man looked at him from under bushy eyebrows across the counter. Lark caught the faint pungency of bay rum and whiskey. Looks a bit like Abe Lincoln, with that long hair and round beard. Wonder if he's as honest, Lark thought. Through the open door behind, Lark could see a flatbed press, fonts of type, a composing stone, and stacks of cut paper.

The man put his hands flat on the counter and said in a dour voice, "I'm Thomas T. Toney, sole prop of the Acheron *Argus*. You are in great need of some job printing, I hope?"

"No, but I'm here on business. I'm Justin Lark, Mr. Toney. I ran across your last week's *Argus* at the Morris House, and say, you put out a dandy little paper. Accept my compliments." Lark was intentionally effusive. "Could I sign up for a year's subscription for your little gem? Send a copy each

36

week to Carpenter Ranche—that's r-a-n-c-h-e—Enterprises, in care of Samuel Eames, 364 Champa, Denver, Colorado."

Toney scribbled down the address. He said, "That'll be four dollars, Mr. Lark. I know that's steep, but everything's high, postage, paper—"

"No, no, the price is reasonable for a newsy journal like the *Argus*," Lark said. "I've got a notion to—by God, I will! Make that a five-year subscription, sir." A gold double eagle thudded to the counter. "No, no, hold it—ten years." He added a second gold piece.

Toney's bloodshot eyes went wide at this unexpected largesse. "Why, I appreciate this, Mr. Lark. Most generous, sir. Many of my subscribers want to pay in due bills or tough beef or chickens—or promises. Coin of the realm is therefore most welcome. I'll take care of yours immediately."

"Thank you," Lark said. He leaned forward, spoke confidentially, "Word will get around soon enough, so you should have it straight from the horse's mouth. I'm land manager for Carpenter Ranches of Colorado. Mrs. Carpenter is in Acheron with me. We're interested in making some—well, substantial investments in Hardup County. If we can find suitable properties, you understand."

"Say, that will make a front-page story," Toney exclaimed. "I must get an interview from Mrs. Carpenter."

Rubbing his jaw as if speculating, Lark said, "Mr. Toney, if—uh, our plans are revealed too soon it might cause difficulties. For now, how about just a little teaser, that Mrs. Carpenter and her Enterprises are looking for land in this area? Then in following issues we'll give you enough news to fill your front page, give 'em both barrels, as it were."

"Say, that would be better. I can milk the story for three-four weeks, might help circulation. Don't forget me, Mr. Lark. And if there's anything else—"

"By golly, there is! How long have you run this fine paper?"

"Somewhere near five years. Took it over in '84. Turned it into a going concern, then when the Big Die-Up hit, I dam' near lost 'er. She's coming back now, thanks to improving conditions, and some—er, substantial backing from the community."

"You have back issues of your paper? I'd like to make arrangements to go through them. That way we could pick up some information on land transactions, cattle sales, water rights, weather and such. A paper as assiduously edited as yours is sure to have stories on those things."

"Well, we do cover county happenings quite thoroughly, if I do say it myself," Toney said. "You're welcome to run through my files, though I'm sorry to say they cover only my five years. The former owner of the *Argus* made a lot of enemies. One night a bunch of his opponents took over the place, dragged all the furniture and files out into the street and set fire to them. Then they shot the editor and threw him into the bonfire."

Lark whistled softly. "They play rough around here, eh?"

"They do. I had to start from scratch, with the building, the press, and a few fonts of type."

"Well, too bad about the guy, but five years of the *Argus* will be sufficient for our purpose. I hope, Mr. Toney, your files never suffer a like fate. Like all editors, you must have acquired a few enemies in five years."

Toney gave Lark an odd look. "Some, maybe, but I've kept my nose pretty clean as far as the rough element goes. Damned if I want to get shot and burned out by a bunch of nightriders."

"Discretion is the better part, eh? You're wise, Mr. Toney. This part of the West is hardly tamed as yet." Lark took a hunting-case watch from his fob pocket. He snapped it open. "Hm-m-m, I'm going to be on the go all day. Could I come in some evening to check the back issues? You wouldn't have to stay, I'll lock the door when I'm finished."

Toney looked dubious, then nodded. "Say eight o'clock? I've got a meeting later."

"That will be fine. One more thing, you're the official county printer? Then you must have a map of Hardup County for sale."

"I do," Toney said. From a drawer he took a large printed map. Lark looked at it briefly, then rolled it up. "What's the fee?" he asked.

"Five dollars. But for you—" Toney began.

"I don't have change. Let's make it ten," Lark said, handing the editor a gold eagle.

Toney looked startled, then said, "Why, thanks, Mr. Lark. I'll see you at eight, then."

Walking toward the courthouse, Lark was pleased. Thomas T. Toney may be helpful, with the possibility of more golden boys crossing his counter. I suspect the man is not noted for his crusading zeal. This tough country must have hammered him as flat as a cow chip.

The courthouse was of faded red brick, turreted, designed by some country architect with an eye for uglification. The first floor and basement seemed to be occupied by the sheriff's office and jail. Lark went up the stairs and found the office marked COUNTY ASSESSOR.

He unrolled his map and laid it on the counter. An attractive young woman at a desk looked up from her work, smiled and stood up. "Can I help you?" she asked.

"I hope so," Lark said. "I'm Justin Lark, land manager for Carpenter Ranche Enterprises. We need a good deal of information on land ownerships, tax rates, roads, and other pertinent data on Hardup County. We thought we might obtain it from Mr. Mordecai, the assessor."

"Mr. Mordecai is—er, not available, Mr. Lark. Since I'm alone here, I'm afraid I couldn't fill such a large order."

"You are Miss Kate Muldoon? Miss Muldoon, I had no thought of having the work done here. But perhaps you could do it at home on your own time. You would be well paid, I assure you. Say fifty dollars?"

Her eyes widened. "Why, that's generous. And I could really use the money."

"Please say yes, Miss Muldoon. They tell me you know a sight more about land in these parts than anyone."

"I should, I learned it the hard way," she said, and Lark caught a trace of bitterness. "I should ask Mr. Mordecai, I suppose."

Lark shook his head, smiling. "It's none of his business, is it? We prefer to keep our plans confidential for the moment, Miss Muldoon, as they concern Hardup County. I'm sure you are discreet. And we'll pay in advance."

"As you wish. If you'll tell me just what you need . . ."

Lark told the girl in some detail what he wanted. Frowning the girl said, "I think all that is available. I'll mark up your map for you. But it will take three days, maybe four."

"That will be fine, Miss Muldoon. Mrs. Carpenter and I have a good deal of other preliminary work to do. Let me know at the hotel when the map is ready."

Lark met Diane at the hotel at noon and reported progress. After lunch they went to see the horses Diane had chosen, and Lark approved them. Samson, a big sorrel, appeared strong and intelligent. The other, Barnaby, had Morgan blood, and was spirited and yet tractable. Diane closed the transaction and put the bills of sale in her purse. She told the liveryman, "We'll be stabling them with you. They must have the best of care."

"They'll get it here, ma'am," the man said, pleased with his generous tip.

The shop of the local gunsmith was on a side street facing the railroad depot. As Lark and Diane entered a bell jangled, and they could hear the burr of drilling in the back room. It ceased and a man past middle age, wearing a leather apron, came through the archway, wiping his hands on a wad of waste. He looked at them over the top of steel-rimmed glasses.

"You're Mr. Racklin? Nice stock you have here," Lark said.

"Try to supply the best," the man said with pride. "What can I do for you?"

"We need a couple of rifles. Saddle guns, repeaters, not too heavy but still powerful. Reliable but accurate is the ticket."

Racklin unlocked a case. He took down a carbine and handed it to Lark. "See what you think of this. It's the newest—Model 1886 Winchester, calibre .45-90. Center fire, nine-shot magazine."

Lark hefted the rifle, then lifted it to his shoulder. He worked the lever, the lock clicked smoothly. He lowered the hammer with his thumb and laid the rifle on the counter. "A beauty. How does she shoot?"

"I sighted her in at fifty yards. Here's some groups made from a bench rest. Used to be able to shoot clusters like that freehand, but the eyes ain't what they once were."

Lark stared admiringly at the groups of overlapping holes in the paper targets. "She's accurate," he said.

"And that new Winchester action is danged near foolproof," Racklin said. "But there's one drawback—she ain't cheap."

"This gun is the one I want, just the same,"

Lark told him. "And Mrs. Carpenter here will have one just like it."

"Kinda heavy ordnance for a pretty young lady like you, ma'am," Racklin said.

"I want a weapon with authority, Mr. Racklin," Diane said. "A rifle that will knock over a running coyote at two hundred yards."

Racklin's eyes twinkled. "Whether the coyote is on four legs or two, eh? All right, I have the twin to this one. But we'd better shorten the stock a trifle." He made some measurements while Diane held the Winchester in firing position. He pocketed his tape measure. "That'll be better. I'll get right on it."

With ammunition, cleaning equipment, and leather saddle boots, the total was sizable. Diane paid from a large roll of bills. Racklin gave her a receipt and said, "Guess you need to carry shooting irons, if you're going to pack around that kind of mazuma in Hardup County."

"This country is rough and tough and hard to curry, eh?" Lark asked.

The gunsmith's reply was drowned out by the noise of the arrival of the westbound passenger, with a clang of bell, a screech of brakes, and a hissing of steam. As the train ground to a stop, Lark and Diane turned to watch through the window of the shop. A few passengers were coming down the steps to the platform.

Now from the end of Main Street came a cavalcade of riders. In front rode a big man on a magnificent black horse accoutered in silver-mounted gear, saddle, and bridle. The man wore a

43

somber black suit, a white shirt with a string tie, bearded, Lark thought, like the pard. His retinue, all on excellent horses, were rather flashily dressed in black, like a uniform. Lark sensed an arrogance in their manner as they scanned the waiting people at the depot.

The leader handed his reins to an outrider and swung down from the black horse. Another rider reached a large leather suitcase down to the conductor. The conductor slid the suitcase into the vestibule of the Pullman palace car and stood aside as the leader mounted the steps. At the top the man paused, doffing his flat black hat, his iron-gray hair standing out in a halo. He spread his arms toward his followers like a benison. The six men took off their Stetsons and bowed their heads. As the leader disappeared into the Pullman, his escort wheeled their horses and were gone down Main Street. Now the locomotive huffed and puffed, the striped mail sacks were tossed into the door of the mail car, the bell clanged. With a triumphant hoot of the whistle, the westbound was away toward the Rockies, the Cascades, and the Pacific.

"Quite a performance," Lark said to Racklin.

"Yep, The Shepherd has gone to round up a new flock of sheep for New Eden," the gunsmith said, his voice harsh. "God help the poor fools."

"We're new here. Who is this Shepherd?" Lark asked.

The fear that had afflicted Shank Morris was lacking in this gunsmith. In a voice like a growl he said, "The show you just saw was the Reverend Hiram Joshua Danville, better known as The

Shepherd, departing on a recruiting jaunt. He is the self-anointed leader of the religious colony of New Eden. The men in his escort of hardcases are known as the Joshuans."

"What do you mean by recruiting?" Diane asked.

"He takes off now and then to round up a new batch of suckers for his cult. He converts 'em to his crazy beliefs, and herds 'em here to Montana. Gone out to the Coast this time, they say."

"The colony must keep growing, then," Diane said.

Racklin shook his head. "Not by any great shakes. Seems like it ought to, since nobody ever leaves. But them that know say the number stays about the same, month for month."

"Some coming and some going, I suppose," Lark said.

"Maybe. And maybe they don't go," Racklin said. "I've heard that the cemetery at New Eden has plenty of permanent residents, on their mountain-top a few miles from the main ranch."

## Chapter IV

"Racklin is the first person I've met who dares speak badly of the Joshuans," Diane said as she walked up Main Street with Lark.

"Independent as a hog on ice," Lark agreed. "I suppose he's valuable to the Joshuans, to take care of the armament of the mercenaries. So they give him a long picket rope. I'll say this for the Joshuans—they ride fine horses. Did you notice that black Danville rode?"

"He's welcome to that beast. I'd wager the horse is from the Excelsior bloodline. Daddy and I owned a few, but we got rid of them."

"What fault did you find with them?"

"They're handsome enough, and spirited, but some have an aneurism in the throat. If ridden too hard, they die quickly. No bottom, daddy said."

"With that army of his, I doubt if The Shepherd ever has to put his black to the test," Lark said. Then he touched Diane's arm with a warning hand. Four men dressed in the black garb of the Joshuans were coming toward them down the sidewalk. And one of them was Badeye Klaus.

Without hurry, Lark took Diane with him to the blank wall of the building nearby, leaving room for the men to pass. But Klaus stumbled, lurching against Diane. The girl thrust Klaus away indignantly.

"Oh, sorry, ma'am," Klaus said, grinning. He flicked a glance at his companions to be sure his acting was appreciated. "But it's tough to stay out of trouble when you walk with a stupid galoot like this guy."

Lark made a quick survey of the odds. Armed, all of them, he saw, guns hung low. "Pros, able gunmen, or aspiring to be," he said, his voice flat. "That's enough, Klaus. Don't bother the lady. Move along."

"S'pose the lady, if she is one, wants to be bothered?" Klaus asked with a leer. "If I want a bit of conversation with her, you won't stop me."

Lark stepped in front of Diane. He said, "Klaus, you're a good deal saltier than the other day when I gave Blackie Legrand his needings. I suppose having three of your hardcase friends along makes you brave. If you'll stand aside, we'll move along. Good day, gentlemen."

Klaus was taken by surprise as Lark walked with Diane past the four. They were half a dozen paces beyond when Klaus yelled, "You, Lark!"

Lark said quietly, "Into that doorway, Diane. Trouble coming."

Without argument, the girl stepped into the shelter of the doorway. Lark turned. "You want something, Badeye?"

"You need a lesson, Lark. You ain't gonna take

47

me by surprise like the way you did Blackie t'other day. I'm gonna beat the holy hell outen you, right in front of your fancy gal."

Lark smiled coldly. "You wag that lip of yours a lot, Badeye. I'm going to have to feed you that six-gun of yours yet."

The menace in Lark's manner seemed apparent to the other men. One of them put a restraining hand on Klaus's arm. He said something in a low voice.

Klaus shook the man off. "The hell with that," he growled. "You guys don't want to back me, to hell with you. I can handle this ranny."

Lark stood rock-steady, braced, waiting. Klaus saw this. The clubbed fist opened, the hand swept down toward the holstered pistol.

Icily calm, Lark was ready. His hand slid under the lapel of his jacket and came out with the Colt Lightning. Klaus's was still coming up when Lark shot the man twice, once in the shoulder, once in the kneecap. Klaus fired his .45 once, harmlessly into the planks of the sidewalk. The pistol clattered across the boards as Klaus grunted and fell.

Lark's pistol muzzle swung toward the other three men, but none of them made a hostile move. They stood quiet, hands plainly in the clear.

Lark flicked a thumb at the groaning Klaus. "Better get your pal to a doctor, boys," he said. "I doubt if he'll be shooting anyone down in cold blood for a while. And don't hand the law any song and dance about how I drew first on this skunk. Too many witnesses, boys."

"Sheriff's comin' now," the man who had tried

to warn Klaus said. Another of the trio left and came back with Klaus's saddled horse. In spite of the moans and groans coming from Klaus, the other three loaded him on his horse. They led the horse down the street, past the curious spectators who had been drawn out of saloons and stores by the sound of gunfire. The onlookers were strangely silent as the little cavalcade moved on toward the office of Dr. Kermit, the local medico.

Diane joined Lark, a little pale under her tan, her breath coming fast. She said, "Oh, Justin, you're a courageous man! I was scared stiff that abysmal brute would hurt you. Why, you should have killed him!"

"My, but we're bloodthirsty!" he chided. "He had to be stopped, but I don't like killing, Diane. The law turns a jaundiced eye on such goings-on, too. And I do believe the law is coming now in all its majesty."

The paunchy, sour-faced man with the star on his vest introduced himself. "Simon Slagg, sheriff of Hardup County and town marshal of Acheron. Now what the hell—pardon me, lady—is going on here?"

"I'm Justin Lark. Mrs. Carpenter and I were walking along Main Street, minding our own business, when Badeye Klaus tried to pick a fight with me. When he pulled a six-gun, I shot him a couple of times."

"Short and sweet, eh? You kill him?"

"Nope. But I'll wager that slow fast draw of his is finished forever. And likely the man will limp the rest of his misbegotten days," Lark said.

The sheriff's mouth twisted as if he had bitten into something sour. "How d'you happen to be packin' a gun?"

"Why, for self-defense, sheriff. You've got a tough town here. I hadn't been in town ten minutes when Blackie Legrand and Badeye jumped me. I took care of them by hand, then I began wearing a gun for the protection of myself and Mrs. Carpenter."

"You knew these men were Joshuans?" the sheriff asked.

"Why, sheriff, I don't even know who the Joshuans are," Lark said blandly.

"Well, that's no never-mind. Gimme the gun. I gotta run you in for packin' an iron in the city limits, and for assault and battery."

"You'll do nothing of the kind!" Diane cried angrily. "Klaus and the other three were armed— there's Klaus's pistol lying in the street. You just try to make a scapegoat of Mr. Lark, Sheriff Slagg, and you'll regret it. I have friends in Helena in high places in the Territorial government. So if you want to keep on being sheriff of Hardup County, you had better exercise discretion, in spite of the fact Badeye Klaus is a Joshuan."

Boy, this pretty girl knows how to run a sandy, Lark thought admiringly. I'd swear she's a cousin of the governor and a niece of the attorney general.

Diane's act had convinced Slagg, too. He said grumpily, "All right, all right. I won't run Lark in this time. But both of you had better mind your P's and Q's while you're in Hardup County. If you go lookin' for trouble, mister, you're sure as hell gonna find it."

"Why, sheriff, Mrs. Carpenter and I are peaceful, law-abiding citizens," Lark said. "But of course if the Joshuans harass us again, we'll have to take drastic steps in our own defense."

The sheriff's mouth twisted. "There's a good chance you might have to do that. The Shepherd ain't going to like you crippling up two of his men, and that's a gut. You cross the Joshuans again, and all I'll be able to do for you as sheriff is convene a coroner's inquest over your dead body."

"It's comforting to know that my demise will be handled all legal-like," Lark said drily. "Also that the sheriff enforces the law in this county with fairness and impartiality, except around election time."

Sheriff Slagg scowled at Lark, catching the irony in his words, but not sure how to take it. Getting no clue from Lark's bland expression, he said, "Simon Slagg is his own man. I follow the law as she is writ. You or anybody else that breaks the law ends in the hoosegow."

"I appreciate your diligence, sheriff," Lark said.

He and Diane watched Slagg stride away, arrogance in the set of the burly shoulders. The man is sure of himself and sure of the power of the Joshuans, Lark thought. No help for us there, and we'll have to keep a wary eye on him.

Diane brought him back to the present. "Is that the end of it? No arrests, no hearing, no consequences? Just drop the whole thing?"

Lark smiled. "Justice is sudden in cow country, but erratic, lady. People are impatient with long court trials, lawyers wrangling over who is the biggest liar. No red tape when a man gets a hole blown through him, and plenty of times he had it coming. But remember one thing, Diane, never steal a horse in Hardup County, or they'll string you up before the next sunrise.''

In Warner's Harness Shop men were working in the rear. Lark could hear the thump of a foot-powered sewing machine. The man who greeted them was lean, dry and lugubrious. They stated their needs.

''Yeah, I'm Jim Warner. Um, guess I can fit you out. You'll like my saddle, Mr. Lark. 'Montana three-quarter rig' the boys call it, an improved tree of my own design. And Miz Carpenter, I got just the hull for you. Made it for the banker's wife, only she got so fat she couldn't sit it. The Goodnight design, padded horn and leg support, very pretty.''

Diane shook her head, smiling. ''A sidesaddle, Mr. Warner? Not for me. I'll choose your Montana three-quarter too, if you have one somewhat smaller in size than a man's model. You see, I ride astride.''

''Astride? You been with the Wild West shows?''

''No, but I wear copies of the divided skirts those girls wear. I find riding in them more comfortable, and a great deal safer than working cattle or horses on sidesaddle.''

Warner was skeptical. ''Cain't say I approve. It ain't ladylike, nor very dam' modest, either. But that's your concern. It happens I do have a saddle I built for Cheney McRae, out to the Diamond T.

Y'see, Cheney was kinda narrow in the —er, hips. So he wanted his rig jest so. Only he got hisself killed in a gunfight over to White Sulphur, so I'm stuck with the hull. Make you a good price, Miz Carpenter."

The two saddles proved fine examples of the saddlemaker's art. As Diane was counting out the considerable sum needed for the saddles and bridles, Lark praised Warner for his work.

The saddlemaker gave him a thin smile. "I oughtta know a thing or two about my trade," he said. "I worked for Hugh Moran over to Miles for five-six years before I set up my shop here in Acheron. Come because I had a cousin here, Pete Henty. Pete's dead now."

"Is business pretty good?" Lark asked.

Warner gave Diane a receipt and dropped the money into a drawer. "Could be better," he said. "Cash money is just coming out of the tobacco cans and hidey-holes after the Big Die-Up. Along with the rest of the county I pret' near starved for a year or two, but now she's coming back slow."

"I suppose you get a lot of business from a big spread like New Eden."

"From The Shepherd and his Joshuans? Don't make me laugh, Mr. Lark. Them reprobates has all their leather goods shipped in from Keyston in Frisco, Mueller in Denver and the like. Center-fire rigs. I get a patching job on New Eden harness onst in a while, that's all." He spat into the refuse box. "That ain't any skin off my nose, Mr. Lark. I'm like Tom Racklin, I don't kowtow to Danville and the Joshuans. But we're about the only ones in

53

Acheron who don't."

"They pack a pretty big club, eh?" Lark asked.

"Yeah. The Shepherd is like the guy in the poker game with the big stack of chips in front of him, he calls the play. And most of our locals go along with The Shepherd."

"But considering the state of the cattle markets, where does Danville get his money?"

Warner leaned forward, his voice low. "You ain't the first to wonder that, Mr. Lark. But it don't pay to answer questions, even when you're guessing. A lot of folks who did are under stone markers in the cemetery."

Lark gave the saddlemaker a long look. "Of course we didn't hear you say anything, Mr. Warner. But I'm curious. I'd like to read the names on the headstones at New Eden."

"Not likely you'd get in. They got a four-strand bobwire fence around the whole place, and patrols. Only ones get in are the sheriff, and Dr. Kermit and Grady the banker, besides the Joshuans, o' course. Don't ask them three anything, Mr. Lark. They're so deep in The Shepherd's pocket they can't see daylight."

"Suppose a man cut Mr. Glidden's patent barbed wire and just rode in?"

"He'd get hisself killed, most likely," Warner said grimly. "My cousin Pete and his son tried that and they turned up dead. The Joshuan patrols, they say, have orders to shoot trespassers on sight, and they've done just that."

"They must have valuable stock, to need such strong security."

"Their *stock* runs on two feet, not four, the moccasin telegraph says. People from other states, rich people—it's a hell of a thing, Mr. Lark. I only wish—" He was interrupted by one of the workmen who came from the back room to ask a question about the piece of leather he carried. Warner did not resume his sentence. He said, "Thanks for the business, Miz Carpenter. I'll hold your merchandise until you pick it up."

"Tomorrow or the next day, and thank you," Diane said. The door bell jangled faintly behind them as they went out.

Lark looked at his watch and the two walked down the street toward the restaurant. Diane said in a worried voice, "Justin, the more I hear about New Eden the more frightened I become. The girls and Von—this affair has such a sinister ring. Everyone around here walks scared, too. There must be some way to get in there and learn the truth."

"You are right," Lark said. "But we can't move in the dark. We might blow the whole investigation, might get people hurt. I'm hoping we have enough information in a couple days to put some of the jigsaw together and begin planning our moves. I'm praying your kinfolk are still in control of their own assets. They're safe enough while they hang tough about turning over the money. But once their fortunes are in the hands of the Shepherd . . ." He shook his head. "God knows what will happen to them."

"Oh, Justin, those poor darlings! We've got to save them."

"We will, Diane, we will," he said, sounding more confident than he felt.

The small frame house where Kate Muldoon lived alone might have been transplanted from a New England village. The house, painted white with green trim, sat surrounded by flowers within a neat picket fence. Lark tried to estimate the hours of labor involved in carrying water from the well in back to grow the poppies and calendulas and roses that splashed warm color about Kate's yard. He knew it must not be easy for flowers to flourish in the hot sun and desiccating air of a Montana summer.

Lark checked the street in both directions. They had not been followed, so he held the gate open for Diane. Kate Muldoon came out on the porch, made the same wary survey, and welcomed them. When they entered the house, she closed the door behind them, though the evening was warm. She ushered them into her parlor, in which the lamps were lit and the shades drawn.

Lark made the introductions. Diane said, "I truly appreciate the way you are helping us out."

"You seem such nice people I'm glad to do it," Kate Muldoon said. Then a smile illuminated her pretty face. "Besides, I need the money."

"I take it your county salary is not exorbitant," Lark said.

"Hardly," she said. "Mordecai, the assessor, gets the salary and I do the work. So I'm saving for a stake to get me out of the godforsaken town. I want to move away, to Butte or Helena, sell this house

56

and pull out. I couldn't even plan that until my mother died last year—she couldn't, or wouldn't, think of moving."

"I'm sure there's plenty of abstract work in either of those places," Lark said. "But as you say, it would take some capital." He looked at her keenly. "Are you sure there aren't other reasons for leaving Acheron?"

The girl laughed without amusement. "You're psychic, Mr. Lark? Yes, there's a man who won't let me alone. One of the Joshuans, Monte Marshall, captain of The Shepherd's ragtag army. I'm desperately afraid of the man."

"He's from New Eden? I understand that The Shepherd and his Joshuans pretty much run Hardup County."

"You heard correctly. And Marshall—I don't know why he keeps after me. He has two wives already."

Diane gasped. "You mean he wants you to commit bigamy?"

"Plural marriage, the government called it when they barred it down in Utah," Kate said. "Yes, they practice it in New Eden, without interference, it seems. But let's go to something more pleasant. Here's your map, Mr. Lark. It will tell you a good deal about Hardup County and the New Eden."

The map of Hardup County was spread on the kitchen table, the ends weighted with cleaver and sadiron. Lark leaned over it, finding Kate had marked it very professionally, the irregular blocks filled in with different colors.

"I've outlined in blue the ranches that have changed hands in the past five years," Kate said, pointing. "The WIT ranch, there; the Mullanphey spread, there; Coors and Conklin, there; and the J Up and J Down. All part of New Eden now."

"New Eden is the large pink block, eh? What happened to the owners you mentioned, Kate?" Lark asked.

She shrugged. "Gone, left the country, disappeared, dead. Mrs. Carpenter, I'm afraid there is no land in the vicinity that would meet your specifications. All the decent bottom land and good range, the water, and the foothill pasture, belongs to New Eden. Except—" she pointed to a block shaded green, at the south edge of the pink area. "That's Circle H, the Henty ranch. Danville wants it because the Hentys have a right to six hundred miner's inches of water from Malpais Creek. But the Hentys who are left won't give in to him."

"So the Hentys might sell to me," Diane said.

Kate Muldoon shook her head. "I doubt that. There's only Mrs. Henty and a grandson, Danny, left. And Elnora Henty's hate for the Joshuans is worse than her hate of hell. She'd do anything to block Danville, so she'd be afraid a third party might be only a surrogate for him. Her hate is a fiery, consuming thing—the Joshuans killed her husband and her son, and took the son's widow into New Eden, saying she was converted to their strange beliefs. She's now the second wife of Monte Marshall, the man I'm being sought by."

"How strange and terrible," Diane breathed. "It is hard to believe there can be plural marriage in this day and age."

"No more than plural murder, and kidnapping, and perjury," Kate said bitterly. "Why, The Shepherd himself has six wives, and is constantly looking for additions to his harem."

Lark asked a question intentionally vapid. "Is there a chance Danville would sell Mrs. Carpenter some of his holdings?"

Kate's mouth dropped open in disbelief. "Danville wants to expand his empire, not reduce it. He and his Joshuans live like Oriental potentates. The disciples do all the work in the name of expiation and atonement for their sins. Among them harmony rules—The Shepherd's harmony. No, Mr. Lark, when Danville has gathered in all Hardup County, he'll reach for Pine County, his eventual aim the whole new State of Montana."

Lark whistled softly. Diane looked at him, then asked, "Kate, where does the money come from? It must take large amounts to buy more land, to keep New Eden running, and to suborn the law on such a large scale."

"Mrs. Carpenter, Hiram Danville is a most persuasive man. He uses his strange hypnotic power to make converts, and he chooses wealthy ones. They come and turn over fortunes to the man, as they disappear behind his fence."

"Don't some of them become disillusioned?" Diane asked. "How can he keep control over so many?"

"I'm not sure, beyond the discipline of the sect,

and the force of his own magnetic personality," Kate said. "And of course the brutal persuasion of the Joshuans, who are handpicked, brutal men. They say The Shepherd doles out the new women converts to his henchmen to secure their fortunes."

"Oh, my God!" Diane exclaimed. "If that—" She went silent as Lark's hand clamped cruelly on her shoulder.

"From what you say, Kate, people simply don't leave New Eden," Lark said.

"No. Once they are in the colony they seem to lose all will. The most common avenue of escape is to the cemetery high on Mount Moriah, a few miles west of the New Eden compound."

"The death rate is high?" Lark asked drily.

"Very. The discipline of the Joshuans is strict. There are some strange suicides among the disciples. There have been investigations from time to time, requested by relatives, but it is a perfect Eden that Danville shows the visiting officials. Everybody vaguely smiling, happy, no complaints, all for one and one for all. The men and women are busy in the big kitchens, or the fine airy barns among the sleek cattle and horses, or praying in the beautiful chapel with its holy paintings. Never a discouraging word, never an objection. Being a slave is better than being whipped or worse. The disciples accept their lot like—like stupid sheep."

Lark said, "Kate, we've been hearing strange rumors about New Eden ever since we came here, but you're the first one who has given us facts. Are you sure of your information?"

"I am. Mordecai, my boss, and the sheriff, Simon Slagg, and Bulson, the county attorney, are all in Danville's pocket. They let things slip now and then. Monte Marshall, my nemesis, has been very frank at times, pointing out the advantages of being the third wife of a Joshuan. He's not an awfully bright man, so I pump him about New Eden. But I'm afraid of him, I don't know how much longer I can hold him off before he takes me by force."

"He wouldn't dare!" Diane gasped.

"Oh yes, he would. The Joshuans are arrogant in their power. They are so strong now I do believe it would take the U.S. Army to dislodge them."

To tap this gold mine of information, Lark and Diane talked with Kate for another hour. Before they left, Diane paid Kate her fee and added another fifty dollars. Kate demurred, but Diane insisted the work was worth it.

"And if you need any help with this Marshall character, don't be afraid to yell for me," Lark said. "I'll fix his clock for him, the same way I did Legrand and Klaus."

"I heard about that. Good for you, Mr. Lark," Kate said. "But Monte Marshall is more dangerous than either of them, so watch out for him."

Going to the door with them, she paused, a hand on the knob. She looked straight into Lark's eyes. "Tell me the truth—you two are doing more than landlooking, aren't you? It's New Eden, isn't it?"

Lark smiled and touched the girl's cheek with his fingertips. "Kate, for a pretty girl you are damned smart to boot. Let's say for now that the influence of the Joshuans is one of the factors involved in the purchase of our proposed ranch. So we must look into it very deeply."

Kate Muldoon nodded in understanding of what he had not said, and let them out. As they went down the walk they heard the snick of a door bolt being thrown on the cottage door.

## Chapter V

Lark was lost in thought and silent as he walked with Diane Carvell toward Main Street past the scattered silent houses.

"Danville is the key," he muttered to himself.

"What did you say, Justin?" Diane asked.

"Oh, nothing much. Digesting what we learned tonight. Trying to find an end of string to unravel this cat's cradle of a case."

"What's our next move?"

"I should go over to the *Argus* and check Toney's back issues, but I'm not in the mood. I've already stalled him a couple times, another night won't hurt. Why don't we ride out tomorrow to the Henty ranch? I want to have a look at the place and talk to the old lady."

"That's fine. I'd like to see some of the range country. This ugly town is giving me the willies. Let's get an early start and carry a lunch."

"You weren't joshing when you told me you knew horses," Lark said, reaching down to pat Samson's sleek neck. "I like this fellow, I'll bet he can go all day and half the night.''

Lark and Diane were riding west from Acheron in the slanting sun of early morning. Meadowlarks sang sweetly, a crow cawed raucously. From far off came the faint moan of the engine whistle on a Great Pacific freight, its direction lost in the sweep of distance. The horses trotted along a poorly defined track through scarred buckbrush and green-gray sage. The air was cool, but the flawless sky promised heat later in the day.

''Thank you, Justin,'' Diane said. ''Samson and Barnaby weren't the first horses I looked at, I assure you. I think they'll serve us well in any situation.''

The girl riding beside Lark wore a daring divided skirt over polished boots, a plain shirtwaist and a leather jacket. A small hat with a jaunty feather framed her short curly hair. Her skin was summer gold, and would, Lark thought, grow even darker in the actinic sunshine of this altitude. He nodded approvingly at the .45-90 Winchester in her saddle boot. I'd bet if it comes to fire-fight this pretty damsel will handle herself well.

''What did Mr. Eames have to say in the night letter you got this morning?'' she asked.

''Not as much new information as I had hoped,'' Lark said. ''He said Hiram Danville is quite well known, half preacher, half health zealot. Complaints from the relatives of some of his disciples have come to nothing. No dope available on New Eden from the Territorial attorney in Helena.

64

With the sect money Danville has available, the top officials may be in The Shepherd's pocket, too."

"And in this wicked country, if Danville's purse of bribery fails, a gunshot is faster than a gavel," Diane said angrily. "Has Mr. Eames learned any more about that plural marriage business?"

"He's picked up more rumors confirming what Racklin and Kate Muldoon told us—that it is a definite practice of the New Eden sect."

"Could New Eden be an offshoot of the Mormon religion?" Diane asked.

"Definitely not," Lark said. "In fact, the Latter Day Saints have come down hard on polygamy, in the hope of being granted statehood next year. Eames learned that a prominent Mormon family had filed a complaint that Danville had kidnapped their son. But the Territorial officials in Utah found the young man was of legal age, had gone with The Shepherd of his own free will, and did not want to return to his family. That closed the investigation, though I'm sure the family wasn't satisfied."

Diane was silent, her head bowed, for some time. Then she cried out, "Oh, God, Justin, what of my sisters? Two beautiful, wealthy young girls lost in that horrible commune without anyone to turn to? What if they were forced to marry? What is the Montana law about a wife's own estate?"

The trend of her thought jolted Lark. He pushed back his Stetson and scratched his head. He said slowly, "I wish I was sure. There's joint tenancy of land and other real property, so I would think the wife would keep sole title to whatever else she brought into a marriage. But how the courts would hold in the case of a bigamous marriage, I can't guess. On top of that, there's a constitutional convention sitting in Helena this minute, in preparation for Montana statehood this fall. Only God knows what that bunch will write in it about inheritance. If they go with the old common law, the husband is the absolute master of his wife's body and all she possesses."

"If Danville could make a bigamous marriage stick through his bribed judges, then he could seduce my babies, or give them to his henchmen, and after—after they were—dead, he'd get their estate. Oh, Justin—"

"He'd do away with the girls to inherit? Don't panic, Diane. A bigamist would know he was getting a branding iron with the hot end if he tried that, and maybe a noose. Just keep your shirt on, lady."

"But there's no word from them! Maybe they're already—" She spurred her horse and raced ahead of Lark up the long hill facing them. He let her go, knowing she was fighting for control of her dread. When he joined her at the top of the hill she had recovered a measure of calm.

She swept an arm toward the wide coulee below them. A weathered forlorn house sat in a grove of cottonwoods beyond a sparkling creek. "That must be the Henty house," she said. "Let's pay them a visit." Lark nodded, and kneed Samson

66

down the hill toward the creek.

The house had seen better days. Paintless, unkempt, with one broken upper window stuffed with rags against the wind. The porch sagged from a post rotted at one corner. In a pole corral two horses sought the shade of a rickety barn. A few chickens scratched industriously in the duff of the barnyard.

Lark and Diane rode through the shallow ford and through the open gate. A large dog of nondescript breed was lying on the porch. He raised his head, a growl rumbling deep in his chest. As they came nearer, the dog stood up, his hackles bristling.

The screen door flew open and a woman stepped out on the porch. She was thin, wearing a dark dress with an apron tied over it. She held a Spencer repeater at the ready across her chest.

"We'd like to talk to you," Lark said.

"I won't have the likes of you on my land. I got nothing to talk to you about, so git." She raised the rifle menacingly.

"But we're friends," Lark protested. "Mrs. Carpenter and I want to talk about buying your ranch."

"You were sent by them devils from the hell they call Eden, damn you! Murder wa'nt enough for 'em, so they try this way to git my place. I ain't sellin', I ain't talkin'." The woman's voice was harsh.

"But madam—" Diane began.

The woman whipped the rifle to her shoulder.

"If you won't understand plain talk, mebbe you'll understand hot lead. I said git, and you git!" The Spencer cracked and the bullet raised a gout of dust almost under the belly of Lark's horse. Samson shied and Lark had to quiet him.

"She means business," Lark said. "We'd better pull out."

Diane nodded. She wheeled her mount and they rode through the gate. Lark, looking back over his shoulder, saw the woman standing defiant, the big dog at her knee. She did not move, challenging them until they rode south through the brush along the creek.

They came to a widening of the trail and Lark halted his horse. He took off his Stetson and wiped his brow with his wrist. He said, "Whew! That old gal doesn't mince words, does she?"

"She was like a mother bear protecting a cub," Diane said.

They rode on again, the trail now shadowed by brush, now open where the creek bent away. They rode out of a grove of aspen to see a large pond, the water glittering in the soft breeze. A young boy was standing at the water's edge, intent on his fishing.

"Hey, young feller!" Lark called.

Instantly the boy dropped his makeshift pole and dove for the rifle leaning against a bush. Lark held up both hands, palm forward. "Hold it, son," he called. "We mean you no harm. How about a bit of palaver? I'm Justin Lark and this is Mrs. Carpenter from Denver. We're land-looking."

Holding a battered .22 rifle, the boy straightened. He looked at them with suspicion written taut on his freckled face. About twelve, Lark thought, tough and wiry and old beyond his years. Bet he's never seen a girl as pretty as Diane, he's intrigued by her. "Talk to him, Diane," he said softly.

The girl swung down from her horse and passed the reins to Lark. As she approached the boy, he could see she was unarmed, and he grew less tense.

"I'm Diane," she said. "How's the fishing?"

"Purty good," the boy said, managing a faint smile. Putting down his rifle, he reached into the water below the bank. He lifted a willow withe holding a fine string of perch, bluegills and crappies. "Enough for a meal or two for me and gramma." He replaced the fish in the water. Wiping his hand on his ragged overalls, he extended it to Diane. "Pleased to meetcha, Miz Carpenter. I'm Danny Henty. You sure you ain't got any truck with New Eden, or The Shepherd?"

"Danville? I assure you we do not, Danny," Diane said earnestly. "In fact,—but I'll let Mr. Lark tell you about it."

She's winning the boy over, Lark decided, and dismounted. He tied the horses to a bush and joined Diane. He said, "I'm Justin, Danny. She's right, the Joshuans and me, we don't jibe. Twice they braced me in town. One of 'em tried to bulldoze me, and I threw him out in the street, maybe busted his shoulder. Later another of 'em tried to pull down on me and I shot him a couple of times. Tall guy was called Blackie Legrand and

69

the chunky one Badeye Klaus."

"You tackled Blackie Legrand?" There was awe in the boy's voice. "And Klaus? You kilt him, I hope."

"Nope, but they won't be worth much for quite a while, neither of 'em," Lark said. "You know those two, Danny?"

"Yeah, too well. They're two of the Joshuans' bully boys. They were the ones—say, you better keep your back to the wall from now on, Mr. Lark—Justin. And don't ride at night. The Joshuans will have it in for you."

"I've handled a few hardcases in my day, Danny, and those two didn't seem too tough to me," Lark said cheerfully. "You live around here, son?"

The boy pointed. "Along the crick a mile or so, me'n my gramma." With a note of pride he added, "The two of us run our own spread, Circle H."

"Your grandmother wouldn't be a thin lady with gray hair who is right handy with a Spencer repeater?"

The boy grinned. "That's gramma. Hey! I thought I heard a shot a while back. Run you off, did she?"

"She sure did," Lark said ruefully. "She told us to git, and when we didn't move fast enough, she unloaded a warning shot. We didn't stop long enough to argue aye, yes, or no."

"She don't trust nobody, gramma don't. I'm purty much the same way, after all we've been through. I shouldn't be talking to you folks, but if you tangled with The Shepherd's men, you must

70

be all right."

"An enemy of theirs is a friend of yours, eh, Danny? We don't know much about that bunch, only rumor. Got time to give us chapter and verse?"

The boy glanced at the sun, at the bobber on his fishline, and screwed up his face in thought. With some reluctance he said, "Mebbe a little. It ain't a pretty story, and it ain't over yet." His eyes narrowed and his jaw set. "Nor it won't be over, never, until I settle our score with The Shepherd and Monte Marshall."

He's just a boy, but there's an iron ruthlessness in him, Lark thought. The Joshuans must have put the Hentys through hell. And this boy wants desperately to talk about it to someone who will listen.

While Lark and the boy found seats on a downed sapling, Diane went to her horse and took something from the saddlebag. Coming back, she gave Danny a generous helping of chocolate bar. He eyed it wonderingly, then took a bite, and another. With his mouth full, he said, "Hey, Miz Carpenter, I ain't never et nothing that tasted so good."

"Take all of it, Danny, and enjoy it," Diane said. "It will help wet your whistle for your story."

"Golly, I don't hardly know where to begin," the boy said.

"Clear back at the beginning, Danny. How did New Eden start?" Lark asked.

"Well, that was afore my time," the boy said

71

seriously, and Lark concealed a smile at the old-man expression. "But gramma has told me about how some folks come out from Indiana and built their new Eden."

"They were a religious sect?" Diane asked.

"Yeah. Good people, gramma said, but peculiar in their ways. And that had got them in trouble back home, so they come West and took up land, some fifteen years ago. Good people, gramma said, didn't harm nobody. The Hentys, grampa and gramma, my dad and mother, they got along fine with the Edenites, as they called themselves. Their land run west of us, to the mountains."

"How much land, son?"

"Land was dirt cheap then, they had about two thousand acres of boughten land, and then each couple homesteaded their half section and deeded it over to the whole bunch. Y'see, in their religion nobody worked for hisself, everything belonged to them all. They shared everything."

"A commune," Diane said.

"I guess so. Anyhow, they run into trouble, with Indian renegades, and drought, and hoppers, and bad winters. They found this wasn't farming country, like they was used to, and they didn't know sic-'em about ranching. But what really licked 'em, gramma said, was one of their religious ways. Men and women got married, but they wasn't allowed to—uh, you know what I mean. Anybody did, and had children, they got run out of Eden. So as them Edenites got older, there wasn't no kids to help work the ranch, nor to take the place of the folks that got old and sick and died. So about seven-eight years ago, the colony was on its last legs."

"Not the first commune to fail because of a rule of continence," Lark said to Diane. "Go ahead, Danny, we want to know more."

"Well, the old man who was The Shepherd, and the rest, they sent back to Indiana for new younger people to join up and come. Pump in new blood, gramma called it, a mighty long shot. But the Edenites had faith, and sure enough, along comes maybe twenty young men and women led by Hiram Danville. Danville claimed he was Joshua leading his chosen people to Jericho, and first thing we knew, he was ramrodding the New Eden."

"And what of the original elders of the colony?" Lark asked.

Danny shrugged, his eyes remote. "They—well, they faded out. Guess about the only one of 'em left is a crazy old guy named Elihu Noon. He was one who took up with the new ways Danville ordered, like a man and wife ought to breed children, even that a man could have more'n one wife."

"You know this for true, Danny?" Diane asked, frowning.

"Oh, sure. Gramma said The Shepherd found it easier to convert women than men, so when he brought the disciples to New Eden he didn't have enough men for husbands for 'em, so he made this new rule. He doled 'em around even to the hired guns he brought in to keep the disciples in line and hard at work. 'Course, the young pretty ones he kept for hisself, they say The Shepherd has six wives already."

Diane cried, "But that's illegal. That's polygamy. How does he—?"

"Get away with it?" Danny's laugh was mirthless. "The Shepherd is his own law. His whole spread is fenced, and patrolled night and day by his Joshuans. Nobody gets in or out of New Eden without his sayso, I tell you. Sheriff Slagg and Doc Kermit get called in onst in a while, but mostly to certify that some pore devil died from 'natural causes.' Gramma says Danville owns every official in Hardup County, and when he says 'Jump!" all they say is 'How high?'"

"And people who hold out against Danville?" Lark asked.

"If he can't buy 'em with money the disciples bring in, they are likely to have accidents. Thrown from a horse, shot in a saloon brawl, house burned down at night—things like that. New Eden has twenty thousand acres now, and gramma says pretty soon they'll own the whole county."

"Danny, how have you and your grandmother been able to hold out?"

"We got an original water right Danville wants, but that's gov'ment law, so he can't fake a title. Oh, I s'pose he'll come it over us one of these days, but until then me'n gramma will fight."

"I heard your father and grandfather are dead," Lark said.

"Murdered. By the Joshuans," the boy said

74

bitterly. "Then the devils took my beautiful mother to New Eden. She's married now to Monte Marshall, his Number Two wife, damn him."

Marshall again, Lark thought, remembering Kate Muldoon. He asked, "Was your mother taken by force, Danny?"

"They said she went willing," Danny answered. "Mama was a city girl, and she was tired of livin' poor on a scratch-gravel ranch, and sufferin' and losin' in the Big Die-Up couple years ago. Then she lost a baby and began actin' real strange, lettin' everything go, spendin' most of her time just sittin' and readin' her Bible. Monte Marshall got next to her some way, maybe when us menfolks was gone and gramma was in Acheron nursin' a sick woman. Anyhow, one day mama was gone, leavin' a note sayin' she had heard the word of Jesus, and gone to join the true believers of the New Eden."

"Your father and grandfather went after her?"

"Yep, took their guns and cut the bobwire fence, and rode for the colony headquarters. They made me stay with gramma." The boy's voice was hoarse with rage and regret. "Me'n gramma found 'em two days later—both dead. Shot. Layin' where the cut fence had been fixed."

"How awful!" Diane exclaimed. "Did the law do anything?"

"Nothin'. Slagg claimed they had an argument and shot each other, just like Cain and Abel. Nothin' gramma and me could do about such a dam' lie."

"They've left you alone since, those Joshuans?"

"So far. Gramma says when Montana becomes a state this fall, Danville will buy a state official or two, and have them fix up things about the water right. Then we'd better look out. It'll be pull stakes or die, one."

Lark rubbed his chin speculatively and looked at the boy. He said, "Danny, that's one hell of a story, and I know it's true. But I've got an itch I can't scratch—I'm betting you know a lot more about the New Eden and the Joshuans than you've told us."

The boy didn't answer directly. "I gotta know plenty if I manage to keep me'n gramma alive. I got my ways."

Lark spun a gold eagle glinting in the air and caught it. He said, "Son, I'm betting you have a way of spying on the doings of New Eden. Ten dollars says you have a secret trail in, and another ten says you can watch what goes on at head-quarters without being caught. You don't have to say what or where it is, just that you have a way."

Lark could see that the boy was tempted, not by the gold Lark was clinking in his fingers, but by the boyish pride of outwitting the Joshuans. Danny ate the last bite of his chocolate bar, looked at Diane, and slowly nodded. Lark dropped the two coins into the fob pocket of the denims.

"Son, we may need your help one of these days," he said. "When we do, we'll holler. Until then, you and your grandma must play your cards mighty close. Don't say a word to anyone about our talk."

"I got to tell gramma," the boy said.

"Of course you do. Tell her Mrs. Carpenter and I are friends, so she'll leave the hammer down on that Spencer the next time we come."

The boy grinned, and gave Lark a small callused hand. "I'll tell her. Anybody that bucks the Joshuans has to be a friend of ours."

# Chapter VI

After they left the boy, Lark turned Samson east, and they forded the creek in a sheet of diamond spray. They were still well south of Circle H as they climbed the hill to intersect the weedgrown track to Acheron.

"The kid knows plenty," Lark told Diane. "I was a kid once, I remember how kids like to brag. Danny came mighty close to telling me he has spied on headquarters, perhaps seen his mother."

"Then he may have seen the girls and Von," Diane said, her voice touched with excitement. "I must ask him, Justin."

"After we've prepared the way," Lark said. "One small boy can't do much, even for his mother's sake. And if he took me in there—the way things stack up, that might be plain suicide. Diane, I've got to holler for help. Action against New Eden will take more than the two of us. This is no simple piddling gang, they're ruthless and well organized. What we're getting into is war, full scale. I'm going to tell Sam Eames."

"If this was Colorado, I could stir things up,"

Diane said. "I know some important people, including the governor. I would pull some strings."

"But this is Montana, with all the big bugs deep in the political turmoil that attends becoming a state. There are some outsiders who can help, though. I'll have Sam try to put some pressure on them."

"Who do you mean, Justin?"

"The Federal Government. Our big chief, Allan Pinkerton's successor, is in Chicago. The government owes Pinkerton's plenty. Chicago will try to get Washington to move in some U.S. marshals. There would be an excuse, since polygamy is now a Federal offense."

Diane was silent for some time, then asked, "Justin, who is the top man in Chicago, in your Pinkerton office?"

"All I know is that he began as a regular op and worked up. He prefers to be nameless. In our Pinkerton code he's 'Uncle Allan.' But he packs power, lady, so I think we'll see some U.S. marshals on our side soon."

When they reached Acheron in mid-afternoon, Diane went to visit what shops the town afforded for notions and necessities. Lark shut himself in his stuffy hotel room to compose a long progress report to Sam Eames, with his call for help. He folded and sealed the letter, stuck on a two-cent stamp, and put the envelope on the desk. He leaned back, scowling.

His proximity the last few days, and especially on the ride this morning, with a beautiful, intelligent girl had not developed any romantic attraction for her. Instead, Diane's presence had whetted his loneliness. He and Sonya had been apart now and then in the years of their married life, and every time he had missed her horribly. And now there was little Sammy, who Sonya said was the spit and image of his father, but her claim was denied by an adoring Justin Lark, who hoped the child would be as handsome as his mother was beautiful.

All this he poured out now in a letter to his wife. He told Sonya more than he had Eames. "I feel as if I were trying to break into a coconut with a quill pen," he wrote. "Danville's New Eden is fenced in as tight as a cannonball safe. I'm scratching for ways to tackle the situation, without much luck. I've hollered to Sam for help. The Carvell kids, and others, are in real danger." He described seeing Danville, and the manner in which he had arrived at the railway depot with his armed retinue. "It was a show, like a prince of the blood surrounded by his courtiers and his bodyguard. We learned he was on his way to the Coast, Portland and Seattle, to gather new disciples for the colony. Each acolyte with a pocketful of money, of course."

He concluded his letter by telling Sonya how much he missed her and the baby. He did not dwell at any length on Diane Carvell or their association, for though he had nothing to hide, Sonya Verloff Lark had the fire and temper of her Polish ancestry, and Lark had no desire to suffer her wrath.

In most towns, the U.S. Mail was inviolate, but Lark was not sure that would apply in Acheron. He walked down to the depot with his two letters, and when the eastbound train came in, he dropped the letters into the mail slot of the express car.

Thomas T. Toney called to Lark, "Come on back here, Mr. Lark." Lark raised the hinged flap on the counter and went through to the pressroom. Toney wiped his inky fingers on a rag already dirty and doffed his apron. "*Argus* goes to press tomorrow, but I'm about finished," he explained. "Hey, I'm running the story about you and Mrs. Carpenter. See what you think of it."

With a hand roller he pulled a proof of part of the locked form on the composing stone. Lark read the smudged page and smiled. Toney had written a teaser story, keeping it quite mysterious in tone. He nodded approval.

"Thought you'd like it," Toney said. "That will give all of Hardup County an idea of what you're after, then next issue I'll give 'em both barrels, front page stuff. You want the back issues?"

"If you don't mind," Lark said.

Toney waved a hand toward a cupboard. "All five years in there. I've had 'em bound for convenience, though it's damned expensive. You browse through 'em as long as you want. Door's on the night latch, just blow out the lamp and pull the door to when you're finished. I've got an appointment."

When Toney had left, Lark cleared the clutter from a table, moved a kerosene lamp closer, and opened the first big volume. He began skimming through the issues, making an occasional note.

Two hours later he closed the last volume, partial for 1889, and folded his note paper. He blew out the lamp and fumbled his way past the counter. Opening the door, with his usual caution he looked up and down the street before he stepped out. He pulled the door shut behind him, hearing the latch click. He strode through the dimness toward the hotel, staying close to the building fronts, though Acheron was immersed in its usual glum stolidity.

In the Morris House, Lark nodded to Mrs. Shank Morris at the desk, and went up the stairs. He unlocked the room door, checked for any intruder, and crossed the room in darkness to pull the window blinds before he lit the lamp. Acheron sure stretches a man's nerves, he thought.

Unrolling the map Kate Muldoon had prepared, Lark began fitting his notes to the properties on the map. He found a picture forming, plain as a blueprint developing in its bath of potassium dichromate. At the time Toney had begun the *Argus*, Hiram Danville was just consolidating his hold on New Eden. Things began to happen, things that enabled the colony to spread east and north as an octopus enveloping his prey.

At first Lark had found a few mentions of New Eden, and Danville, and the Joshuans. Then all references disappeared. In Vol. I, No. 1, was the story of the death of Jens Johnson of J Up & J Down, shot to death by persons unknown. Later issues told of the sale of the ranch by the Johnson heirs, buyer and price not specified. But Kate's map showed the ranch now a part of New Eden.

A year later the bachelor Mullanphey brothers died in the fire that destroyed their ranchhouse. The ranch was sold, price not given. The map showed it in New Eden. The next spring Dave Weatherall of WIT was bucked from a horse thought to be gentle and broke his neck. Sold for back taxes, WIT was now a part of New Eden. Another year, Abe Coors and Slim Conkling, partners in the CC Ranch, quarreled and killed each other in an unwitnessed gunfight. The two widows sold out and fled the county, price not given. But again the map showed the CC now part of the New Eden holdings.

Perhaps all the violent acts Lark had gleaned from the *Argus* had not had their origin with the Joshuans, but the evidence pointed to Danville's people in many cases. Homesteaders had been burned out. A halfbreed had been lynched on small provocation. The elected sheriff and one of his deputies had drowned while duck hunting, the bodies never found. Percy Allard, the county treasurer and recorder, had died from eating bad oysters. Strangely, others who had eaten shellfish from the same cask had suffered no ill effects. Strangely too, both the sheriff and the treasurer had been replaced by Danville men.

No wonder, Lark thought, the people of an area half the size of Connecticut are in fear of their lives. No wonder they won't talk. It will take a mighty challenge to The Shepherd's power, something forthright and successful, before these people will join to defeat the Joshuans.

The classic method—that's the ticket. Infiltrate as deeply as possible, make the ringleaders suspicious of each other, suborn some dissatisfied or greedy underlings. Stir things up, disturb the chain of command, keep the top men off balance. Then at the right moment, move in on the gang in force, with the law behind you. It has worked before, it will work again.

Easy to say, Lark thought, but putting the plan into operation is a pinto with different spots. The ideas which had been taking shape in his mind had no body as yet, nor could he do much against the Joshuans and Hiram Danville until help had come from Eames.

He tossed the pencil down and rolled up the map. Time for bed, he thought. Maybe my dreams will tell me something. It wouldn't be the first time that happened.

As the days passed, Lark's frustration grew. In their role as landlookers, he and Diane visited the ranches in the path of New Eden expansion. The story was the same everywhere, at the Cross 7, the Rail Fence, the Anchor. People tight-mouthed, suspicious, obviously worried but not about to talk. Cattle operations had not come back to normal after the terrible winter of two years before. The market was still low, land values not out of their slump. They had to gamble, to use their credit to build up herds, to bring in better sires. The hope was that a few seasons of good weather and good grass, plus a rise in beef demand, would enable these ranchers to make a comeback before their loans were foreclosed. Meantime they rode with a Colt at their belt and a Winchester in the saddle boot. These ranchers would not, Lark found, answer even the most discreet questions about New Eden.

Lark woke one morning to find the sky overcast and a chill wind driving down from the north. He dressed warmly and waited in the lobby for Diane. As they walked to Kate Muldoon's for breakfast the coolness was welcome after the summer heat.

A few days before, Kate Muldoon had said hesitatingly, "Would you and Mrs. Carpenter consider taking your morning and evening meals with me? I'm better than a fair cook, and my rates would be reasonable. I thought you might be tired of risking ptomaine at the restaurants."

Lark said, "Kate, we don't need the second shake of a lamb's tail to take you up on that. Not only will you be a good Samaritan, but we can hold our councils without being suspected of plotting against The Shepherd."

"I thought of that," Kate said, smiling. "I don't know what you two are up to, but I'm sure you're on the side of the angels. You've given me new life just by being here in Acheron."

"You're a sweetheart, Kate," Lark said. "Now, I could use a bit of information. Are the station agents trustworthy? I must send and receive some telegrams, business matters, you know, and I don't want the contents spread all over Hardup County."

"Especially in certain circles," Kate said. "Yes, I think both men can be trusted, though Clyde

Jarvis might tip Tom Toney off to a news story now and then. But old man Osweiler, on the night trick, is like a clam. Nobody will get anything out of him even if they use the Chinese water torture."

"My thanks, Kate, I'll send my wires at night, then."

The change in weather seemed to have lightened Kate Muldoon's mood this morning, for she hummed a little tune as she served Lark and Diane hotcakes and bacon, eggs from her own chickens, and powerful coffee.

Finished, Lark leaned back, replete. He said, "Kate, you're always pretty, but this morning you reflect the bonny bloom of youth."

"Git on wid your blarney, ye spalpeen," Kate said. "'Tis no way for a man to tease an old spinster of twenty-eight." She dropped the Irish brogue and said seriously, "But something has happened. Dr. Kermit shipped my boss, Joshua Mordecai, off to Miles to the hospital. And Mordecai won't be coming back, terminal, Doc said. Oh, folks, I hope you won't think me heartless and unfeeling, but I have no pity for Joshua Mordecai. He's a mean, conniving, miserly man and he has had his hand in some dark and vicious plotting."

"We can't blame you," Lark said. "Sometimes people deserve exactly what they get from life. Is there a chance you'll be appointed assessor?"

"Justin Lark, are you crazy? Not only am I not in the circle of the Joshuans, but I'm a woman. No, I suppose I'll continue to do the work while someone else has the title and the pay. But when my stake is big enough—"

As Lark and Diane entered the hotel after breakfast, Shank Morris called to Lark. "Mail for you, Mr. Lark. Came in on the westbound. Looks important."

"It is," Lark said. "Deed forms, bills of sale, stuff like that."

The hotelman's ears pricked. "You about to buy some land?"

"Could be," Lark said. "Come, Mrs. Carpenter, we'll go upstairs and get to work on these. It took your associates long enough to send them."

While Diane waited impatiently, Lark made sure the large manila envelope had not been tampered with. He cut it open. Several sheets from Eames which Lark put aside, with hectograph copies of telegrams the agency head had sent. There were two unopened letters in identical envelopes addressed to *Miss Diane Carvell, 1680 Larimer, Denver, Colorado*. Lark noted they were both postmarked *Acheron, M.T.*

"Oh, I know that handwriting!" Diane cried. "They're from the twins." She tore one open and read quickly. Her face paled. With a sob she handed the letter to Lark. The Spencerian script read:

> *Dearest Sis:*
> *I have been chosen to be the beloved wife of the finest man who ever lived, the man who has donned the mantle of Jesus Christ to save the world's sinners. I eschew my misspent years and am now at peace in the*

*glory of the Lamb, awaiting the great day.
The ceremony that joins me with The
Shepherd will take place as soon as he
returns from Seattle. I wish you could be
there, but you are an unbeliever and you
are not allowed. Still, I pray daily that you
will see the light and share the happiness
soon to be mine.*

*For my dowry I wish to present my
beloved with 100,000 dollars. Using the
power of attorney which you have, have
the bank make out a certified check in that
amount to Hiram Danville. Mail it to me
c/o New Eden, Acheron, M.T. immediately.*
                    *Your loving sister in Christ,*
                                    *Kristin*

Lark folded the missive and put it back in its
envelope. This Danville doesn't mind shooting
the moon, he thought. He waited for Diane to
finish the other letter. He heard her breathe, "Oh,
my God!" Her face was taut with emotion and
tears ran down her cheeks as she gave Lark the
letter.

Lark scanned the letter. The script was more
angular, less flowing, but similar to the other. But
the words, except for the signature *Gracia* were
identical with the wording of Kristin's letter.

"These letters were dictated," Lark said angrily.

"Yes, written under duress," Diane said. "My
dear ones have been made slaves by that lecherous
beast. How can a man with six wives already—
Justin, he wants their money!"

"And since they are pretty, their bodies too," Lark said grimly. "And the sad thing is, with Danville the absolute czar of this region, there isn't a damned thing we can do about it."

Diane's first shock and fear now flamed to anger. "Well, I can do something, and I will. I'll kill this Danville, kill him dead! He's not a saint, he's a devil, debauching young girls, and robbing them into the bargain. And my little brother, God knows what this self-styled Shepherd has done to Lavon."

"Your sentiments are understandable, lady, even laudable. But your first problem is to get at the man to kill him."

She looked at Lark blankly, then a faint cold smile touched her lips. She glanced at the open letter she still held. "I know a way," she said simply.

"You'll manage the barbed wire, get past the fence patrols, evade all the security of New Eden?" Lark asked.

She tapped the letter. "Remember the fanfaron when The Shepherd left on the train? Well, I'll be at the depot when he returns, among the crowd. When he comes down the train steps, I will shoot him dead."

Horrified, Lark said, "Good God, no, Diane! Your life wouldn't be worth a plugged nickel! Though you're a woman, those hellions of Danville's wouldn't hesitate to riddle you with a hundred bullets."

"I don't care. My own life doesn't matter if I can save my loved ones from that beast."

"Oh, don't talk like a damned fool!" Lark said harshly. Grasping her shoulders, he shook her. "Killing Danville wouldn't end this affair. Remember what it says in the Bible—when the devil was exorcised from the sick man, he came back with seven other devils more wicked than the first. There's an empire at stake, Diane. Some Joshuan devil would move in to take Danville's place. Someone just as wicked and ruthless as he is."

She was silent for some time, then she proved Lark's estimate of her intelligence was correct. "You're right, Justin, damn you. It wouldn't help. Just the same, I'm going to be at the depot when he comes back. If I could save some poor soul from his spiderweb of intrigue—"

"Not much chance, but I'd like to be there too," Lark said. "Maybe we'll learn something to help us. We still haven't much to go on. Matter of fact, we don't even know when the man will arrive."

"I intend to meet every eastbound passenger train, until I see that bearded Satan get off the Pullman," Diane said firmly.

"Well then, you'll have until four this afternoon. That's when Number Twenty-Six stops here from the Coast. What say we go for a ride after I've read what Sam Eames has to say?"

Reading the letter from his chief, he said, "As I suspected, nothing good from Helena. Sam says everyone there is in such a dither about statehood nobody wants to bother about our affairs. He's got our Chicago people working with Washington to bring in Federal help, but that's a slow process. He thought the two letters your lawyer had turned over to him might be important."

"And so they were, though they won't bring The Shepherd any of my girls' fortunes. That might help keep them alive," Diane said grimly.

"Right as rain," Lark said. "Listen, Sam ends with a mysterious note: 'You won't approve, but I'm attacking this problem from a new angle. Don't be surprised at a new development.' Wonder what Sam has up his sleeve? He can be devious at times."

"We'll just have to wait and see," Diane said. "Meantime, I'll change into riding togs. Where are we going?"

"Out to Circle H. I'm sure Danny Henty knows a great deal more than he told us. I'm going to see if either of us can pump the lad for further details on the New Eden."

"I'll take along some candy for a bribe," Diane said.

## Chapter VII

As Lark and Diane rode into the Henty yard, the big dog stood up and watched them, not challenging, but alert. Elnora Henty was sitting in the cool of the porch, working the plunger of a butter churn. Not interrupting her work, her free hand strayed to the Spencer leaning against the house wall.

"Morning, ma'am. Could we have a friendly word with you?" Lark asked.

"You're Mr. Lark and Miz Carpenter, ain't ye? Danny told me about you. Well, if you'd like to light and set, I won't stop you." There was wariness in the woman's voice.

Lark tied the horses and he and Diane joined Mrs. Henty. Lark took a seat on the edge of the splintery porch, while Diane sat in a chair next to the ranch woman. Diane said "Here, let me give you a hand." She took the handle of the churn and began the rhythmic up and down motion of the plunger.

"You ain't new to makin' butter," Mrs. Henty said.

"I've done my share of farm work," Diane said, smiling. She reached her other hand into her jacket pocket and took out a paper bag. "Have a chocolate drop, Mrs. Henty?"

Elnora Henty looked sharply at Diane, then reached into the bag. As she chewed on the chocolate drop, she relaxed a little. "My, but it's been a coon's age since I had sweets," she said. "Tastes mighty good." She reached into her apron pocket. "Here, Mr. Lark, you take these gold pieces back. Us Hentys don't ask for charity."

Lark held up his hands. "No, no, Mrs. Henty, Danny earned that money. No charity involved. He gave us information worth many times that to us. By the way, where is the lad?"

"I s'pose he's down to the slough, fishin'. He goes there a lot when the chores are done. Fish is a nice change from chicken and tough beef."

"Danny's a good boy, the very best," Lark said. "He told us the story about his mother. What a terrible thing for the boy."

"A strange, quiet woman, Ruby was, but loving. Maybe Danny don't know, or didn't tell you, but during the bad winter a while back Ruby lost a baby. Took it hard, she did, blamin' herself though it warn't her fault. She took to reading her Bible for consolation, lost herself in it. So she was fair game for that snake, Monte Marshall, and all his holy talk and his wheedling lies. He lured her away, and thereby Pete, my husband, and Bruce, my son, came to their deaths. I hated the girl for a while, but now I just pity her. She's a slave to that no-good Marshall, and the varmint has another wife beside Ruby. It's horrible.''

"Have you had any news from your daughter-in-law?" Lark asked.

Elnora Henty gave him a strange look. She reached into the bag for another piece of candy before she answered. "Well, in a way, but not much. Them New Eden folks is cooped up mighty close. Not there ain't much loose talk floating around, nuther. Death on a black horse rides fast in New Eden, they say.''

"So we've heard, Mrs. Henty," Lark said. He stood up. "Come, Diane, we'll ride down to the slough and have a chat with Danny.''

"The boy likes you, he told me," the woman said as Diane passed the churn plunger to her. "Here, take your candy.''

"You keep it and share it with Danny," Diane said. "Remember, we're your friends. From what we've heard, we don't like the Joshuans much, either.''

The two were almost to the pond when Danny Henty came up the trail, riding a calico pony. His freckled face was serious. "Hello, folks," he said. "Say, I'm in a kinda hurry. Can't shoot the breeze today.''

"We had a chat with your grandmother," Lark said. "She didn't pull down on us with the Spencer this time.''

"Good. She's a wonderful lady, I'm glad you're friends.''

"We are too, Danny. You haven't anything new you can tell us?''

The boy hesitated, licking dry lips. "No, cain't

94

say I have. I was looking for our old brindle milk cow that run off."

"No fish today? Danny, you wouldn't lie to your friends, would you?"

The boy drew himself up defiantly. "S'pose I did know something? It ain't safe for a man to go around spillin' his guts, I tell you."

Lark said to Diane, "Come, Diane, let's ride on. The friend we had at Circle H doesn't seem to be around anymore."

The boy's face crumpled. "Hey, wait up, wait up. I won't—I can't tell you everything. But one thing might prove I'm still your friend—The Shepherd comes back to Acheron on Number Twenty-Six tomorrow afternoon."

"That's something, all right. How do you know, Danny?"

"That's my secret, but I swear it's true. Half the army of Joshuans is riding into town to meet him, and they are taking two surreys."

"He must have gathered in the sheaves," Lark said drily. He put his hand on the boy's shoulder. "I wish you would come clean all the way, son, but I guess you can't. Now remember this, if you bump into anything that's too big for you to handle, get in touch with me or Mrs. Carpenter at the Morris House right away. Friend to friend, Danny. We mean that."

"Thanks, folks, I might—maybe I'll have to take you up on that." He glanced at the sun. "Gotta get going now. G'bye." Kicking heels into the flanks of his lively pony he raced up the trail toward home.

Lark doffed his Stetson and scratched his scalp. He said, "I'd give half the mint to uncover the pipeline Danny has into New Eden. It's just the break we need."

"He'll come around, Justin. Have patience." Diane said. "And if Danville does return tomorrow afternoon, it will be a good test of the accuracy of the boy's source of information."

"Say, that's right. We'll be there, if he doesn't come in this afternoon. Whenever he comes— listen, lady, I hope you've given up the dangerous idea of bushwhacking The Shepherd. You're too pretty to get yourself shot into doll rags."

"Oh, I'll behave," she said, grudgingly. "I spent half the night awake deciding you are right. Killing that beast won't free Von and my girls and the others—there are plenty of other serpents in that Eden. But I tell you, Justin, I'm going crazy worrying about them."

"I don't blame you. I think things will start to move soon," Lark assured her, wishing he were as confident as he tried to appear.

"For whatever that's worth," she said. She turned her horse and slapped a rein end against her boot. "Let's get back to town."

They had just reached the streets of Acheron when the skies opened, and welcome rain poured down over the parched roofs and the parched land. Later, wearing slickers, they waited under the station overhang for Number Twenty-Six to stop at Acheron in the downpour. There was no sign of The Shepherd or of his cohorts, so they sloshed back to the hotel.

In bright hot sunlight the streets of Acheron were drying quickly after the rain. Lark helped Diane pick her way across the streets, dodging puddles, their edges already dry and cracking in the warm wind. The rain had made ragweed and thistle and dandelion in the vacant lots vaguely verdant, new-washed of yesterday's dust. Lark and the girl, passing the harness shop, nodded to Warner, standing in his doorway. He nodded to them.

They angled across the street to the cinder platform of the depot. A number of spectators were ahead of them, joining the ritual of "watching the train come in." Lark found a place in the shade and boosted Diane onto one of the four-wheeled carts lined up to handle the incoming baggage.

"Danny hit the bullseye," Lark said softly. "Look at those two rigs at the end of the platform."

Two surreys were waiting in the stub street. They were bright with varnish, their fringed tops glinting like new-minted gold. The harness of the two matched teams shone. The drivers, lolling on the front seats, were trim in dark trousers and jacket and string tie, their boots polished to a mirror.

"The Shepherd is giving his new flock his most flattering treatment," Diane murmured. "They'll be impressed."

"Their disillusionment will begin when they get to New Eden and have handed over their money," Lark said.

He watched the milling crowd. Through the open window of the depot he could hear the maniac chatter of the telegraph sounder. First chance I get I'm going to learn that Morse code, he thought. It could be right handy to be able to read those messages.

From the west came the wail of the locomotive's chime whistle, two long, long blasts, two short. Along Main Street men emerged from saloons and mounted the horses at the hitch rails. They came riding toward the depot, a phalanx of sleek horses and black-clad men. Lark searched for the handsome black horse of Danville, with its silver-mounted saddle. Not finding it, he concluded that The Shepherd would be riding in one of the surreys today.

Eight of the riders stayed in the saddle, deployed around the surreys. Three others dismounted and pushed their way through the crowd, to station themselves next to the track. Lark recognized one of them and smiled—Blackie Legrand was rigged for a left-hand draw, so the arm Lark had wrenched wasn't good for much as yet. The handsome dude in fancy fringed jacket, silver-mounted belt and holster, with the turquoise ornament on his hatband, Lark pegged as Monte Marshall. The third man Lark didn't know, but he was sure it wasn't Badeye Klaus.

Now the ground quivered and the rails sang. The train came rumbling into Acheron, steam hissing, brakes squealing, bell clanging. The engineer grinned down as he applied the air to stop the Pullman just beyond the depot building.

Lark lifted Diane down from the cart and walked with her to join unostentatiously the crowd waiting near the Pullman steps. The conductor, in blue serge and brass buttons, swung pompously down to place his portable step. A negro porter in spotless white coat helped the passengers at the top of the vestibule steps. The small throng pressed in closer to watch who would get off.

"Get back! Get back, all of you!" one of the Joshuans growled. "Move it, move it! You want a swift kick in the behind?" Lark saw Marshall's hand drop to the .44 in the silver-laced holster. The nearest people moved back precipitately, leaving a clear space of some twenty feet in front of the train, only the conductor and the three Joshuans remaining.

The passengers began to descend the steps. They were an odd group, two older couples, looking dazed, three young girls smugly sanctimonious, two young men, one in a strange cloak of patchwork. Now the bearded one, The Shepherd, followed his docile flock. But he paid no attention to them. Instead he reached up with a fatuous smile to give a hand to the woman who was descending the steps. In a great lacy hat, tall, lovely, she gave Danville her gloved hand and a brilliant smile. Her eyes flicked over the waiting crowd and caught Lark.

He sucked in his breath in shock. It couldn't be—but it was! This gorgeous creature, regal in white broadcloth, smiling like a queen, was Sonya Verloff Lark, his beloved wife.

What in God's name is she doing here? he

thought. He edged forward hoping for a sign, a discreet word, anything. But the bodyguards were alert, their backs to the train. And Sonya seemed too busy chatting with Danville as he handed her down the steps and reached for her hand luggage.

So that's what Sam Eames hinted at in his letter, Lark guessed. Sam couldn't come right out with it, knowing I would have put a stop to it. Nor would I put it past Sonya to have proposed to worm her way into the confidence of The Shepherd. Well, I can't do anything about it now. If anyone can get away with it, Sonya can, she's a cool operative. But she can't know how deadly the danger is that she has thrust herself into.

Numbly, Lark watched the newcomers escorted to the waiting surreys and loaded in. Trunks were taken from the baggage car and put on the four-wheeled carts. The few entraining passengers got aboard and the engine hooted once, tentatively. Danville, smiling through his beard, was still chatting with Sonya beside the train. The Shepherd stooped for her train case.

From across the street a rifle slammed, and lead skreed off from a car wheel. Another shot, and Monte Marshall grunted, clamped both hands to his belly, and pitched forward like a folding rule to the cinders of the platform. A third shot, and Blackie Legrand spun screaming and fell. Lark wheeled and saw a lace of smoke from a rooftop down the street. He yelled "Get down!" and leaped toward Sonya. Grasping her hand, he drew her over the prostrate Danville, who lay prone with his hands clasped over his head. Lark pulled Sonya

100

the few steps to the shelter of the depot building.

"Justin! Darling, who was it?" Sonya gasped.

"Dunno. Baby, what the hell are you doing here?"

"The New Eden case. Darling, I am ze Countess Sonya Verloff, very rich widow, religious fanatic jus' convert to Edenite sect. I haf already ze Shepherd in ze palm of my hand. I go now to New Eden."

"Sweetheart, you're crazy, but I love you," Lark whispered. "For God's sake, be careful every moment. These are killers. How's Sammy?"

"Very fine, I leave him with Mrs. Eames, who loves him. Justin, I come because I am afraid for you. These 'orrible people have no mercy, zey would do anything if zey know you are detective. Quick, when I am inside, how will I reach you?"

Lark took a long chance. "Try to reach a ranch boy named Danny Henty. Maybe through Lavon Carvell. Protect the Carvell sisters, Kristin and Gracia, if you can. Don't trust any Joshuan—"

"Enough, Justin, he comes," Sonya said, and sagged against him, eyes closed.

The Shepherd burst out of the press around the wounded men, disheveled, his eyes hot and wild. Forestalling him, Lark said "The lady became faint from the excitement. Is she with you?"

"Yes. I'll take care of her now," Danville said curtly and put his arm around Sonya. Lark stepped back.

Sonya's eyelids fluttered and the great dark eyes came open. She smiled archly, "Ah, my shepherd, this man catch me when I grow faint with fright at the shooting. Why did not you catch me, my shepherd?"

"Too busy dodging lead," he said. His voice changed, becoming richly mellifluous. He said to Lark, "Thank you, my man. You may go now." He took Sonya's arm. "Come, dear countess. I think the shooting is over, but we must take no chances. The surrey is waiting, well guarded."

Lark watched with deep concern as The Shepherd led Sonya around the milling crowd and handed her into one of the surreys. Both drivers whipped their teams into motion, and one behind the other, they raced down Main Street surrounded by the cordon of Joshuan riders. Splashing through puddles, the cavalcade turned west at the courthouse and went out of sight.

"And who was that lovely creature you were so solicitous about?" Diane's voice behind him was icy. "Fortunately I'm used to fending for myself, even when bullets are flying."

"Sorry about that, but she's important," Lark said. He took Diane's arm. "Come, let's get out of here. I'll tell you about it later."

He hurried her across the platform, skirting a darkening red pool already swarming with flies. He saw Diane gulp and turn her head away. The two crossed the street, heedless of the mud, to the wooden sidewalk.

A group of men, looking forbidding, blocked the way to the hotel. From the group came Dr. Kermit at a trot, his ample paunch bobbling over the taut cincture of his belt. He went on toward the depot.

Sheriff Slagg stepped in front of Lark. "You see who did the shooting, mister?" he demanded.

Lark shook his head. "Nope, me and Mrs. Carpenter were too busy hunting cover. A rifle, by the sound of it. I did catch one puff of smoke over this way. From the roof of the Mercantile, I think."

The sheriff grunted quick orders and his men spread out, two of them running toward the Acheron Mercantile & Dry Goods store. The sheriff stared at Lark, his eyes cold. "That the sum and total of what you know, Lark?"

"Right you are, sheriff. Should I know more? We were just innocent bystanders, the lady and I."

"I dunno how goddam innocent. I hear you been askin' questions about things that are none of your business. But all right, get going."

Halfway up the street, Diane hissed "You know, Justin Lark, that the gunsmoke came from the roof of the harness shop."

"Shut up, woman," Lark growled.

The hotel lobby was empty, and there was no one at the desk. Lark and Diane raced up the stairs to the seclusion of Lark's room. He raised the window shades, letting them fly up. Shoulder to shoulder he and Diane peered out. Even at this distance from the depot they could see that the crowd had grown. Half the population of Acheron must be on the platform by this time. Distantly, Lark could hear the clang of the locomotive's bell, and a sharp hoot of the whistle, warning the crowd as the train pulled out. Battle, murder or sudden death must not be allowed to interrupt the schedule of the Great Pacific, Lark thought grimly.

Diane Carvell turned toward him, her pretty face still framed in anger. "Now, Justin, confess who that woman was," she said. "And why you dropped me like a hot potato to drag her to safety. You were certainly no gentleman, leaving me to fend for myself."

"That woman, as you call her, is probably the key to saving your brother and your two sisters," Lark said. "She's a Pinkerton operative named Countess Sonya Verloff. She is also Mrs. Justin Lark."

"Your wife?" Diane gasped. "She's posing as a disciple to give us someone inside New Eden? Justin, that's incredible."

"But true," Lark said, frowning. "And I don't like it, it's dangerous as all hell. She and Eames set it up, I suppose, her to go to Portland and pose as a rich widow, easy to convert to The Shepherd's phony religion. Oh, she's a dandy, that girl of mine. She has him eating out of her hand already. And we need her inside. But I still don't like it one bit."

"Yes, she's playing with fire. Danville is no fool, he has everything at stake, and he's dangerous, a killer. With his empire at stake—"

"We're playing for big stakes too, girl," Lark said. "Not money and power, but lives. If anyone can pull this thing off, it's Sonya. She's smart, and tough, and she has the brassbound nerve of a riverboat gambler."

"I pray she'll be able to take care of herself," Diane said. "How will she get information out to you?"

"She'll find a way. On a hunch I told her to watch for Danny Henty. I'm sure that kid has a way of spying on the colony. If she can get to him . . ."

"I'm frightened, Justin. This is like a war, intrigues, spies, shots from ambush. Who do you think did the shooting today?"

"Damned if I know, but I count him as a friend. He rendered two of the Joshuans *hors de combat*, maybe killed 'em. And dang near rubbed out The Shepherd."

"Sooner or later, there will be retaliation, and more people killed. I see now why you misdirected the sheriff from the harness shop," Diane said. "But it wasn't James Warner himself—he was standing in the doorway of the shop both times we passed."

"Yes, but he knows more than he has told us," Lark said. "After things cool off, I'll—"

He was interrupted by a soft tap on the door. He touched a warning finger to his lips and opened the door.

Kate Muldoon slipped in and closed the door. She said breathlessly, "I need the two of you. Diane, you and I will walk straight to my house. Mr. Lark, you come alone, circle around. I told Mrs. Morris just now I had found a deal Mrs. Carpenter might like."

"It's important?" Lark asked.

"Life and death," Kate Muldoon said.

"We'll go," Lark said. "Diane, you have that little deringer I gave you?"

She patted the front of her skirt. "Where no man had better try to search for it. Come, Kate, let's be on our way."

When they had gone, Lark checked his Colt revolver and replaced it in the shoulder holster. He waited impatiently for a few minutes before going down the stairs. He stopped at the hotel desk.

"Did you hear any more about the shooting, Mrs. Morris?" he asked.

The woman's round face under the dyed hair was animated. Acheron had not known such excitement in months. To have a couple of drunken cowboys shoot it out on a Saturday night was entertainment. But to have two of the Joshuans shot down in broad daylight by an unknown assailant was of the stuff of history. She said, "I'll know more when Shank gets back, he's down to the depot now. They say Monte Marshall is dead—that'll make two-three instant widows out to New Eden. And Blackie Legrand is shot so bad Doc expects him to shuffle off this mortal coil any minute."

"Too bad," Lark said blandly. "Sheriff got any idea who did it?"

Mrs. Morris shook her head. "Guess not. I hear the drygulcher shot from one of the roofs across the street, missed The Shepherd, but got the other two. Nobody seen him, and he didn't leave any marks or empty shells."

"I wonder why anyone would try to kill The Shepherd," Lark said.

Mrs. Morris leaned forward. She said in a confidential tone, "New Eden has some enemies,

Mr. Lark. And Marshall and Legrand were mean hogs. Plenty of people had cause to hate them, over cards and women and—well, other things. Somebody paid off a personal grudge, is my opinion."

"I can see that," Lark said. "But it's hard to understand why someone would try to murder Mr. Danville, such a devoted holy man."

He left Mrs. Morris staring after him, completely disconcerted, as he crossed the lobby and went out of the hotel.

All Acheron must be in such an uproar over the shooting no one would take any interest in what Lark and Diane were doing. Nevertheless Lark took a circuitous route to Kate Muldoon's cottage, with a wary eye on his back trail. At his footsteps on the porch the door opened, and Kate motioned him in. She closed the door behind him quickly and ushered him into the small parlor.

To his surprise, the room was filled. Besides Diane, he saw Elnora Henty and her grandson, Warner the saddlemaker, and Herb Racklin, the gunsmith. All nodded greeting except Mrs. Henty, who kept looking down, nervous fingers twisting and pulling at a handkerchief.

Racklin stood up and shook hands. "Council of war, Mr. Lark. Everyone here is agin The Shepherd and his New Eden, and we're dang near the sum and total of the opposition in this neck of the woods. We're here because we've got a problem."

"The shooting?" Lark asked.

Racklin nodded. "Yes. Mrs. Henty—"

"I'll tell my own story, Herb Racklin," Elnora

Henty said harshly. She stood up, the knuckles of her hands white as she gripped the chair back. "Mr. Lark, I kilt them two men. They can hang me for it, I don't care. My only regret is that I didn't git that murderin' Shepherd, too."

## Chapter VIII

Lark was startled, but did not find her story hard to believe. He said, "Good shooting, Mrs. Henty. What brought on your vengeance?"

"'Twas the story Danny brought home yestiddy. When he told me, I lost all holts. I spent half the night figgerin' a way to kill Monte Marshall, and this mornin' I loaded the Spencer. Me'n Danny, we come to town in the buggy, and I done it."

"From the roof of my shop, Mr. Lark," James Warner said. "I told you me'n Pete Henty were cousins. When Ellie came to me, I saw her mind was made up, she'd get Marshall one way or another, even in the middle of the crowd. So I helped her to the roof—thank God my crew was off today. After she shot, I got her down and hid her in the shop until I thought it was safe to bring her here. Ellie and Kate are good friends."

"What happened to the rifle?" Lark asked.

Herb Racklin grinned. "We mixed it in with my stock of second-hand guns in the shop."

"Good thinking," Lark said. He looked from

one face to another and drew a deep breath. He said "The Joshuans won't take this lying down. There will be reprisals. We've got to stick together, and we've got to have help."

"From where?" Racklin demanded. "Slagg's a crook, and the county attorney is tarred by the same brush, Helena is busy politicking, they don't give a damn about us. Our best bet might be to pull out of Hardup County while we're still alive."

"Which none of you can afford to do," Lark said. Could he trust these people? He had to. He laid it on the line.

"Hang tough a while longer," he said. "We'll have help. Mrs. Carpenter, who is really Miss Diane Carvell, is my assistant. I'm an operative of the Pinkerton National Detective Agency, out of the Denver office. We're here to rescue Miss Carvell's two young sisters and young brother from New Eden. So you see we have a stake in this deadly game, a big one."

"Say, that's great!" Warner said. "Can we expect more help from your agency?"

"Yes, I'm sending for more men," Lark said. "Our problem is to keep the Joshuans off everyone's back until those men arrive. If the slightest word leaks out, about me, about Miss Carvell, about Mrs. Henty—"

"I'd take the blame for what gramma done," Danny said stoutly.

Lark put a hand on the boy's shoulder. "I don't believe it will come to that, son. First of all, we've got to get you and your grandmother back to

110

Circle H. Suppose Kate finds some sewing for Mrs. Henty to do. Tomorrow you can load it in the buggy and drive home."

"I dunno that the Joshuans would suspect me," Mrs. Henty said, her voice quavering a little. "I ain't skeered. I done what had to be done, according to my lights."

"Of course you did," Lark said. "But the Joshuans will suspect everyone. We must all go about our usual ways. So you and Danny must get back to your ranch, to take care of your stock. It's too late in the day to leave now, you'll both have to stay until morning."

"I've got room, and the barn for the team," Kate Muldoon said.

"Good enough," Lark said. "Now Danny, the time has come for you to spill what you know. We can't help you or your grandmother unless we have the whole story. What did you tell your grandmother that sent her on the vengeance trail?"

The boy licked dry lips. His glance slid to his grandmother. She nodded approval. Hesitatingly, he began, his story unfolding in more fluent fashion as he warmed to the tale.

Some time before, while hunting for strays, Danny had found a dry wash running under the New Eden fence. Boylike, he had explored, and found he could approach the colony in concealment to a point only a quarter mile away. Then moving from bush to tree to low swale, he could reach the dam which diverted the water of a large pond into irrigation ditches. From this vantage point, Danny could watch the activity around barns and fields and dwellings without being seen. New Eden was an extensive spread, at times looking deserted, at other times teeming with activity.

The boy had made a number of trips into his secret spy hole. He had learned how the disciples worked, each group accompanied by a black-shirted Joshuan foreman. The disciples, white robes hiked up to their waists, worked hard. Once Danny saw a Joshuan strike a disciple and knock him down. The man got up, bowed abjectly, and went back to loading manure on a wagon.

Danny had hoped to get a glimpse of his mother, perhaps a chance to talk to her, but the women disciples seemed to be kept at work in the long garden, doing stoop labor. These green manicured plots were too far away for Danny to dare.

One day a young man in a ragged white robe came toward the dam, cutting weeds. Seeing no Joshuan nearby, Danny took a chance and called to the disciple. The young man looked around fearfully, then worked his way toward Danny. Talking softly, Danny asked the disciple if he knew Ruby Marshall, and if he could smuggle letters in and out from her. The young man said he thought he could, but Danny must also smuggle out letters from him.

On Danny's next trip the young disciple came along, working with his sickle near the dam. He told Danny he had learned Mrs. Marshall was a pious woman who was badly used by her husband,

112

who had other wives. Marshall was one of the top men of the Joshuans, and a violent angry man.

Danny asked the disciple if he had any letters to be smuggled out. The young man said he could not obtain paper and pencil, so Danny promised to bring him writing materials. He told the disciple he could lead him to freedom this day or another, but the young man said he must stay in New Eden to protect his two sisters, who were disciples, too.

"His sisters?" Diane interrupted. "What was the name of this young man, Danny?"

"He called himself Von. He said he didn't deserve any other name, he had acted the damned fool and disgraced it."

"He's my brother!" Diane breathed. "Oh, thank God, he and the girls are still all right. Go on, Danny."

"Your brother? He's a good guy, I saw that. Yeah, he seems healthy, he's thin and wiry. Only thing is, he wears glasses and one of 'em is cracked so he don't see so good, he told me."

The girls were O.K., Von told Danny. They had comparatively easy jobs, kitchen work, slopping hogs and feeding chickens. Being pretty, they seemed to be marked for special treatment, often being called to sing and play the piano and violin for The Shepherd in his private apartment. The Shepherd would gather his six wives around him and fondle them while the concert went on.

Since Von's regular assignment was keeping the weeds down at the reservoir, and clearing the canal gates of trash and debris, he was able to meet Danny often, and keep him informed of activities at New Eden. Von reported that while The Shepherd was away recruiting, the Joshuans were more lax with their charges. But The Shepherd's deputy, a man named Elihu Noon, took The Shepherd's absence as an opportunity to increase the religious fervor of the disciples. A religious fanatic, Noon cared little about the fields and the livestock, he was interested only in saving the souls of the disciples. The hours of prayer grew longer, the hymn singing went on for hours, fasting and penance was the order of the day. Von said everyone was praying for the return of The Shepherd, for under him though life was harsh, it did not match the brutal fervor of Elihu Noon.

But Von's visit with Danny yesterday had brought information which drove Danny wild. First Von had told Danny of The Shepherd's impending return by train the following day, bringing some new disciples. The colony was to prepare for a ceremony in which The Shepherd would marry simultaneously the two Carvell girls, making them wives No. 7 and No. 8. in a few days. Von begged Danny to get help from somewhere, anything to stop this farce. He himself was helpless in the face of the Joshuan's power.

Then Von told of an incident which showed the absolute dependence of the disciples on the whims of the Joshuans. Apparently Ruby Marshall, Danny's mother, had refused to sleep any more with Monte Marshall. Marshall had dragged her into the dining hall, and before the gathered disciples, he had stripped her naked. Then he had whipped her with a quirt until she collapsed bleeding and unconscious. He ordered the disciples to take her back to his quarters, an example of a wife who disobeyed her husband.

It was this news that angered Danny to the point where he could hardly talk to Lark and Diane when he met them, though he did tell them when the Shepherd would return. At Circle H, he told his grandmother, swearing that he was going to kill Monte Marshall regardless of consequences. Mrs. Henty had calmed him down, but planned the trip to Acheron. She herself had wrought the vengeance on Monte Marshall.

"I killed the sarpint," Mrs. Henty said with satisfaction. "And Blackie Legrand too, the man who murdered my husband and my son. Woulda got that hypocrite Danville too, only he stooped down and I missed him. Only had three ca'tridges."

"You sure made those three shells count, Ellie," James Warner said. "Legrand ain't dead yet, they say, but with Doc Kermit tinkering with him he'll be ready for Boot Hill by morning."

"Ain't the first varmints I ever shot," Elnora Henty said. "Herb Racklin, I want that Spencer of mine back just as soon as it's safe. Cain't tell when some other varmint might come prowlin'."

"You'll get it, Ellie. I'll find a way," Racklin promised.

"Lark said, "Mrs. Henty has clipped two birds

115

out of The Shepherd's army, but he has plenty left. We aren't in a position to start a shooting war. I've sent for help, but until it gets here, we'll have to lay low and hold our fire. And we need more information on the setup out there at the colony."

They talked for another hour, with Diane, in dread over her kinfolk, advocating boldness, a confrontation. But she was alone, and cooler heads prevailed over her impassioned pleas. When the two town men had gone, Diane was angry at them and at Justin Lark.

"I just can't let a client get herself killed," Lark said.

"Just the same, when you ride I'm riding with you," Diane said.

Lark did not argue. He said, "Since you Hentys are staying with Kate tonight, Diane and I will leave as soon as Danny and I have taken care of the team. Come along, son."

Though there was still a glow of twilight, it was dark inside the barn. Lark lighted a lantern and hung it on a nail. By its yellow light he and Danny fed and watered the Circle H team and Kate's saddler.

When the chores were done, Lark said, "Let's have a talk before we go back, Danny, man talk. The women don't need to hear it."

They sat down on a hay bale and Lark put an arm across the boy's shoulders. He said, "You've been playing a man's part, son, and you'll have to keep on doing it. What I must ask you to do will be dangerous."

"I ain't skeered, Mr. Lark," the boy said. "I'm ready to do anything it takes to get my mama away from them dirty Joshuans."

"Good man," Lark commended. "Now, even your grandmother must not know about what you and I are planning. One slip by anyone and the fat is in the fire, and maybe you and I and others will die. Now listen closely, son. A woman came with The Shepherd today, who calls herself the Countess Verloff. She will pretend to be a disciple, but she's a Pinkerton agent. For God's sake, don't take the slightest chance of blowing her cover, or she's dead. She knows about you, she'll try to get information to me through you. So here's what you must do . . ."

Later, when he blew out the lantern and went back to the house with Danny, Lark was satisfied. Danny was discreet, and would set up the link from Lark through Von to Sonya. A tenuous link at best, but it would have to serve until more operatives arrived.

Diane's manner was distraught as she walked back to the hotel with Lark. "Those devils, those rotten devils!" she exclaimed. "Justin, if that bigamous marriage of my darlings must be stopped."

"I'm sure my wife will figure out a way to do that," Lark told her. "Sonya is tough and resourceful. Your two virgins won't be deflowered, she'll see to that. Sonya might even make The Shepherd divorce the six wives he already has!"

"It's not a joking matter," Diane said sharply.

117

In his room preparing a long telegram informing Sam Eames of the latest developments, Lark was tempted to read the riot act to Sam for sending Sonya. But he decided that satisfaction would wait until he met Eames face to face. Moreover, he wasn't entirely sure Sonya wasn't the moving spirit in that bold plan. He knew his wife was impatient for action, after the long wait with the baby, and Lark's several absences on cases.

A rap came lightly at the door. One—pause—two—pause—one. Pinkerton code, Lark knew, and grinning, went to the door. Just the same, the Colt Lightning was in his hand as he unlocked the door.

He said softly, "Why you old son-of-a-bitch!" and catching the arm of the man who stood in the hall drew him inside. He relocked the door and thrust his pistol back into the shoulder holster.

"Sam Eames said you needed a guardian to keep yourself from getting killed," Art Rankine said.

"That's close enough to scare a man," Lark said. "I wouldn't want a better man to side me than you, Art. Not after the Stoneman's Gap fracas. How have things been going?"

"Fine as frog's hair. You knew I sold the Rank and File saloon in Magma a year or so ago, and signed up with you Pinks. Well, I haven't had a dull moment since. And Sam says this tangle in Acheron is a dilly."

"She's a peacherino, all right," Lark said. He was more than pleased to have Art Rankine to back

118

him up. The ex-marshal of the tough mining town of Magma had steel nerves under a calm manner. He knew the criminal mind and was fast and accurate with rifle and pistol. "Magma was pretty tame without the Redtops gang, eh?"

"Dull as dishwater. Most of the action is at the Gap, where the railroad is coming through. You heard from the Tetraults?"

"Yes. Con tells me Rimi had twins last fall. I think he misses his job as a Pinkerton, though he and Rimi are busy enough at the Inn."

"Yeah, he's a good man, Con is. Bet we could use him here." Rankine rolled a Bull Durham cigarette and lit it. "Well, Justin, what's the pitch on this New Eden business? Sam didn't have time to tell me much."

Lark ran through the story of the case, including today's shooting at the depot, and the arrival of Sonya Lark. Briefly he recounted Danny Henty's involvement. "Art, the whole affair has been like punching a featherbed, until now. But with a link to the colony, and Sonya on the inside . . ."

"That wife of yours has the nerve of a government mule," Rankine said. "She's in a damned dangerous spot, but she can handle it."

"If she doesn't get caught getting a message through," Lark said, frowning. "The Carvell boy is the weak link in our chain. I'm going to try to have Danny take me into the colony to talk to Von. Art, I wish we had someone else in New Eden to back up Sonya."

Rankine leaned back in his chair, eyes half

closed, blue smoke dribbling from his nostrils. He rubbed his jaw speculatively. Then he stubbed out his cigarette and leaned forward. "Justin, remember Frank Flaherty, the boozefighter who was my deputy marshal in Magma? I ran him out of town after the Redtop deal, and I heard he got into a mess of trouble after that. The grapevine tells me he's in the pen at Walla Walla under another name. Suppose Frank Flaherty from Magma put in for a job with the Joshuans? By his record, Frank is tough and mean and crooked enough to qualify for a hired gun."

"You, Art?" Lark asked. Rankine nodded. Lark hesitated, then nodded. "It might work. Danville needs to bolster his army, that's a gut. I'd sure sleep a lot better if I knew you were there keeping an eye on Sonya and the Carvells. But it will be all-fired dangerous."

"If Sonya can hack it, I guess I can," Rankine said. "How'll we work it?"

"Simon Slagg, the sheriff, is as crooked as boar's piss on snow, and he's hand in glove with the Joshuans. He hangs out at the Silver Dollar. Let's stage a bit of a brawl there tomorrow, about second drink time. Mix it up good—you'd have to win, of course. Slagg will break it up, giving you a chance to get chummy with him."

"Say, it will give me a chance to get in a few good licks on you," Rankine said, grinning wolfishly. "Don't you pack a gun. But I will, and when I pull down on an unarmed man, after you're licked, that'll prove to Mr. Lawman I'm the kind of hard-to-curry ranny Danville is looking for."

"You've got it, son," Lark said. "But try to pull your punches."

# Chapter IX

Lark found the Silver Dollar well filled when he entered near midday. He paused a moment as the batwing doors whuff-whuffed shut behind him, to survey the crowd. Good, there will be plenty of witnesses, he thought, to testify to Art's cantankerousness. And there's Slagg at a table, playing cards. Cutthroat euchre, no doubt.

As Lark walked past the table, Slagg looked up and scowled. Lark scowled back, and kept on to the end of the long bar, where Art Rankine was talking to the bartender. Rankine had one boot heel hooked over the brass rail, and was wearing a holstered pistol slung low at his side. Slagg enforces the no-gun rule more in the breach than the observance, Lark decided.

Elbowing in beside Rankine, Lark ordered beer. When it came he took a sip from the tall mug and set it down. He waited until Rankine had his whiskey glass almost to his lips, then he turned suddenly, his elbow spilling the beer mug, the beer splashing Rankine, and a bumped elbow spilling the whiskey.

Sputtering, Rankine put down his empty glass and dabbed ineffectively at the wet front of his vest. He growled at Lark, "You clumsy bastard! I think you done that on purpose!"

"I didn't, but if you're in the mood for calling names, I'll try again. Bartender, another beer."

"Pretty goddam smart, aintcha? You could be breedin' a scab on your nose, mister. Where I come from, people have learned to walk mighty soft around Frank Flaherty."

"You're a long way from home, then, Flaherty," Lark said coldly. "You look like pretty small potatoes to me."

"Lookin' for trouble, eh? I do believe I'll oblige you," Rankine said, turning to face Lark.

Without a word, Lark ripped a right hand into Rankine's middle. The man grunted and sagged forward. He gasped, "Why, you ornery pilgrim! You're gonna get yours, right now!"

Both men had played the fake fight game before. Blows were slipped, or checked at the the last inch. Grimaces and grunts and oaths studded the performance, played to an enthusiastic half-circle of saloon patrons. Now Rankine miscalculated a looping right and caught Lark on the nose. The resulting gout of crimson gave more proof of the legitimacy of the fight, though Lark could have done without it.

Then Rankine winked, and swung a mighty roundhouse right that caught on the shoulder close to the chin. Lark went down into the stale sawdust of the floor and lay there, groaning. Rankine stepped close and kicked Lark hard, only the two of them knowing the boot toe stopped in sawdust. Now Lark leaped to his feet, grabbed Rankine, and kneed him in the groin. Rankine knocked Lark down again. As Lark stared up at him, Rankine pulled his pistol.

"I'll kill you for that, you skunk!" Rankine raged, and pointed the gun.

"Here, here, no shooting!" Sheriff Slagg yelled, and seized Rankine's arm. "Gimme that six-gun, afore somebody gets hurt."

Rankine stared at the sheriff, then as if seeing the badge for the first time, he let down the hammer of the pistol and handed the gun to the lawman. "He had it comin'!" he said. "But I wouldn't want to cause trouble for you, sheriff."

Slagg stuck Rankine's gun in his belt. "Got an ordinance about packing iron in town. You can pick your gun up at my office in the courthouse."

"I'll do that," Rankine said. "I know what you're up against, sheriff. I was a lawman myself, deputy marshall of Magma, Montana Territory. Name's Frank Flaherty. Ain't one to make trouble, but I meet it head on when it comes. This bastard—" he swung a hand toward Lark.

Lark lurched to his feet and brushed sawdust from his clothes. He snuffled, wiping blood from his nose with the back of his hand. "Well, you didn't have to be so damned sudden, Flaherty. It was an accident, I spilt the drinks, and I was ready to buy another when you started the name calling. You didn't need to get so ory-eyed, but I'll forget it if you will."

"I don't forget a deal like this, mister," Rankine

said curtly. "Just stay out of my way from now on."

"All right, all right, I'm leaving," Lark said. He walked to the doors and out, ignoring the derisive glances of the onlookers. He went to his hotel room to clean up. A good performance, he thought, though hardly worthy of a Booth or Barrymore. Nor did that damned Art need to be so realistic with that punch in the nose.

When he took Diane to lunch, he made no mention of Art Rankine or their little comedy. Diane told him she and Kate Muldoon had gotten Mrs. Henty and her grandson safely off to Circle H. Tragedy was no stranger to Elnora Henty, and she had put behind her any guilt feelings over the deaths of Monte Marshall and of Blackie Legrand, who had died during the night. Mrs. Henty had told Diane and Kate, "I never had no regrets over shootin' coyotes that was after my calves and chickens, so I don't regret shootin' them two-legged coyotes. Not after the things they done."

"Good work, kid," Lark approved. "Danny will have a chance to scout New Eden soon, maybe tomorrow. I want to be there when he returns. He might have some message from Sonya."

"You're worried about her safety, aren't you, Justin?" Diane asked.

"Worried as all hell," he admitted. "And about Danny and Von, too. If any of them get caught, the Joshuans will crucify them. But we've put our moccasins on this track, there's no turning back now."

"I certainly will not, Justin," Diane said tersely.

Then she smiled wanly. "I find a kind of grim amusement, though, in the thought of my spoiled darlings cutting weeds and butchering chickens and slopping hogs. They are learning something about the real world."

"They are that," Lark agreed. "The hard way. You want to ride out to the Henty's tomorrow? Maybe we could sneak the old gal's Spencer back to her, too."

"Try and ride without me," Diane said.

Lark checked at the hotel desk on "Henry Smith" a code name used by Pinkerton operatives. Shank Morris shook his head. "Checked out a while back. Gonna catch the train, I expect. Seedy lookin' gent, I take him for a whiskey drummer, or a minister that lost his pulpit. You know him?"

"Thought I might have, but I didn't." Lark turned away. Art Rankine had checked out, which meant he had caught on with the Joshuans. Now Lark had two strings to his New Eden bow, and best of all, an able man to give protection to the Countess Sonya Verloff, heart of Lark's heart.

Then a thought struck him and he turned back to the desk. "Shank, you mentioned a parson. It just came to me that I haven't seen a man of the cloth in Acheron, barring The Shepherd of New Eden."

Morris looked around fearfully. Then he said in a low voice, "We used to have, Babtist and Lutherian. But both of 'em sermonized about New Eden. The Babtist got killed in a runaway, and the Lutherian pulled up stakes when his wife was found in Madame Lou's whorehouse. Claimed she was dragged there by three men, but the woman couldn't make it stick, so they left town. Since then there ain't neither preacher nor service, God help us."

The bitter bile in his throat was a physical sickness as Lark turned away. Is there any limit to their vileness? he thought. He had been determined before but now his resolve turned to steel. If it were humanly possible, he would destroy utterly Hiram Danville and his New Eden.

Lark and Diane rode out to Circle H on a bright sunny morning, the shimmering heat waves blurring the mountain peaks to the west. Diane had left her own .45-90 at Kate's, and slipped into her saddle boot Mrs. Henty's Spencer rifle. When she gave it to the woman, with a box of cartridges, Mrs. Henty smiled grimly. She patted the rifle's scarred stock.

"Thanks, Miz Carvell," she said. "I felt kinda lost without it. A body never knows when coyotes might come prowlin' around. Say, Danny ain't here. He promised me he'd git here by noontime, and the sun says it's about that. Got a batch of bread just out of the oven. Would you like a bait of bread and cold milk?"

They had hardly finished the crusty warm bread, generously spread with new-churned butter and drunk their sweet milk, when the clatter of hoofs announced the arrival of Danny's paint pony. Danny was so excited, so exhilarated by the challenge of danger, he was hardly able to eat the bread and drink the milk his grandmother brought him. His words fairly tumbled over each other until Lark held up a palm and cried "Whoa!"

The boy looked at him, grinned, and gulped milk. He said more calmly, "I seen Von. He's gonna talk to the Countess Verloff on the sly, tell her he can smuggle a letter out, but to be awful careful."

"Good man. Danny, I'm going with you tomorrow. I've got to see the layout of the colony for myself, and there may be a note from Sonya. You think you can sneak me in on your secret trail?"

"Easiest thing in the world, Mr. Lark. We should be there by nine, Von goes to work then, after breakfast and two hours of prayin' and singin'."

"I'll be here in plenty of time," Lark said. "Anything else?"

"Yeah, Von sent a message to you, Miz Diane. The wedding of your sisters to The Shepherd has been postponed. Mr. Danville spends most of the time chasin' the Countess, he'd do anything for her, Von says. She's got the prayin' down from six hours a day to four, and the grub is a sight better. He says everybody in the colony is grateful for the Countess, 'cept maybe some of the Joshuans."

"Thank God for her," Diane said fervently. "My little idiots are saved for the moment. Danny, has Von said anything about what the disciples are thinking? Whether the members of the cult believe the teachings of The Shepherd any longer?"

"He told me he don't believe any of it anymore,

128

nor his sisters, but most of the others—well, they're as bad as when they came. They claim their hard labor and suffering are in—in—what do you say, punishment?"

"Atonement," Diane supplied the word.

"Yeah, that's it. Though they are treated like dogs, the disciples take it all the time without grumbling. The Joshuans even beat them sometimes but the disciples don't fight back or try to run away. Von says that is glorifying the spirit over the flesh. He said they had to pray extra hours for Legrand and Marshall, but nobody was sorry them two were gone."

"Has The Shepherd appointed a new segundo in Marshall's place?" Lark asked.

"Yes, Von says a man named Elihu Noon. He was one of the old Edenites, he turned when The Shepherd took over. He's the real thing, Von says, lots of prayin' and chantin' and hard work. Noon wants everybody to live in poverty until the final day of glory. Von and the rest are scairt of Noon. Von calls him a fanatic."

"Danny, has Von mentioned Badeye Klaus?"

"By gosh he did. They buried Klaus a few days ago, he had some kinda accident and died."

"I'll bet," Lark said drily. "Crippled, he was no use any more."

When they had thanked Elnora Henty for lunch and ridden away, Diane said "Justin, I'm going with you and Danny tomorrow. I must see—"

"You want to sign a death warrant for two boys?" Lark said harshly. "I'm taking a chance by

129

going, and three people—we can't gamble, girl. No, you can come and keep Mrs. Henty company while Danny and I are gone. If we don't get back, you can get word to Sam Eames.''

"Don't say things like that, Justin Lark!" Diane cried.

That evening Lark composed another careful telegram to Eames, including news of Rankine's arrival. He took the blank to the depot and handed it to the dyspeptic elderly man at the counter. The agent counted the words, spat into the brass spittoon, and said above the clatter of the telegraph sounder, "That'll be a dollar six-bits.''

Knowing some operators let traffic pile up, Lark put a gold eagle on the counter. "Take it out of that," he said. "And keep the change for yourself. This wire is quite important and I'd like it to be in Denver by breakfast time.''

Staring at Lark with faded blue eyes, the agent rubbed a gnarled knuckle across his white mustache. He glanced down at the golden coin, smiled tautly at last and said, "Gotcha, mister. Your man will have it right after daylight, unless the messenger boy falls off his wheel.''

Knowing the town was still buzzing over the killings at the depot, Lark decided the best place to pick up the current gossip was the Silver Dollar saloon. When he ordered beer at the bar, the barkeep gave him a faintly derisive glance, but said nothing. Lark sipped the cold lager, eavesdropping on the conversation of two cowhands beside him at the bar. Evidently the pair were newly in from the range, for they asked questions of the bartender. He regaled them with the gory details of the shooting.

"But who do they think done it?" one of the riders asked.

"Your guess is as good as mine," the bartender said. "The sheriff hasn't made a pinch yet, and that's for sure."

"Oh, hell, Slagg couldn't find a blind dog in a butcher shop!" the second man said. "Unless the dog's name was Joshua."

The bartender flicked a glance at Lark, then leaned forward. "Cowboy, I'd button my lip was I you," he said quietly. "Some things better not be talked about around town. Here comes Sheriff Slagg now."

As the sheriff came up, both cowhands became deeply interested in their drinks. Slagg bellied up to the bar. Without a word the bartender unlocked a cabinet above the back bar and took out a bottle with an ornate label. He polished a tumbler and put it on the bar beside the bottle. Slagg poured his own copious drink as the bartender walked away. Lark noticed that the sheriff did not pay.

"How's the bloody nose, Lark?" the sheriff asked, a note of derision in his voice.

"It's coming along. My God, sheriff, that was a hot-tempered son-of-a-bitch," Lark said. "Didn't give a man a chance to say 'Excuse me.'"

"Flaherty is a sudden kind of gunslick," Slagg said, grinning. "He used to be town marshal out of Magma. They say he's killed a few men in his time."

"I'll keep out of his way, I don't want any trouble," Lark said. They've already wired Magma, he thought. Good thing Art thought up that cover story. He added, "Thanks for the advice. I'll steer clear of the guy, though our paths aren't likely to cross again."

"You might run into him sooner than you think," the sheriff said smugly. "He's hired on with the Reverend Danville, The Shepherd, out to New Eden. Them boys come to town every now and then."

"What does a sky pilot want with a man like Flaherty?" Lark asked.

"Oh, he'll use him for this and that, bodyguard mostly. There's plenty of tough monkeys in this part of Montana, Lark, and some of 'em resent a fine, religious leader like The Shepherd. Y'see, he gravels them sinners like hell, and we got lots of 'em. So in case some clown tries to git at The Shepherd, he keeps a squad of faithful men around him."

"I can see why—I was at the depot dodging hot lead myself the other afternoon. I saw two of his men take bullets that were earmarked for The Shepherd. Greater love hath no man, eh?"

"Yeah, it ain't the safest kind of work, I'll tell a man. Blackie and Monte gone, and before that Badeye Klaus. He did hire on your friend Frank Flaherty. The Shepherd told me—" As if he had said too much, Slagg stopped talking. He sipped his whiskey.

"A pleasure talking to you, Sheriff. Can I buy a drink?" Lark asked.

"Why, don't mind if you do," the sheriff said. He poured from his private bottle, while Lark ordered another beer. The bartender charged Lark for beer and drink, but only rang up the beer. Nice little arrangement, Lark thought.

"That's good duty with the Reverend," Slagg said. "Too bad you're so tied up with that Miz Carpenter, you might try for a job at New Eden."

"Good pay, is it?"

The sheriff nodded. "Good pay, good grub, clothes furnished, the best of riding stock. And—" he licked full lips and leaned closer to Lark "—there's some damn' pretty girls among them disciples. The Joshuans have their pick. Y'see, Lark, The Shepherd's eleventh commandment is that the female body is for the enjoyment of man and woman. Sometimes a man might wish he didn't have a wife, so he could sign with The Shepherd." He guffawed and smote Lark's shoulder with a heavy blow.

"But a man with a wife who tried it might get a hole blown through him with a ten-gauge Greener, eh?"

"Hey, you must know my wife!" The sheriff guffawed again.

Lark laughed obligingly. Seeing the good whiskey was mellowing the sheriff, he asked, "They say Monte Marshall was a sort of ramrod of the Joshuans. Who'll take his place with The Shepherd?"

"A buzzard by the handle of Elihu Noon. And t'tell the truth, Lark, me'n Noon don't jibe worth a pile of horse turds. Noon acts too churchy to suit me. I think the man's a dam' hypocrite."

"Wonder if Noon and the new man, Flaherty, will tangle."

"The Shepherd can handle 'em both," Slagg said confidently. "Except maybe he's too busy chasing that Countess Verloff." He chuckled.

"Was that the Countess, that beautiful woman at the depot? She fainted when the shooting started, and I kept her from falling. My God, Sheriff, that's the handsomest female I've seen in all my life."

"From what I hear, The Shepherd has the same opinion. 'Course, he has six wives already, but that makes no never-mind to The Shepherd. Always room for one more, eh?"

"He must be some man," Lark said. "Say, I'll bet the noses of those six wives are out of joint, the way he's chasing the Countess."

"They won't make a fuss—they'd better not. He knows what he's doing, the Countess ain't just pretty, she's richer'n billy hell, too. That title 'countess' is the genuine article, the real quill. She owns diamonds and rubies and such that would put your eye out. Some dame, that one."

"The Shepherd is a lucky man, to convert her to his religion," Lark said. "Well, it has been nice chewing the fat with you. I hope that crazy killer doesn't strike again. Your sheriff job is tough enough without some maniac drygulching people, maybe even trying to drill the sheriff himself."

A strange expression came over Slagg's face. The danger Lark had suggested could not have occurred to the sheriff before. Now the man was reviewing the vulnerability of everyone with New Eden connections, and that must include Slagg and his deputies. There might be a gunman lurking out there right now with a lead slug marked for Slagg. Lark concealed a smile, knowing he had started the wheels turning in the sheriff's head.

The sheriff gulped the last of his drink and took his foot off the brass rail. "Gotta be moving along. Say, Lark—uh, you wouldn't happen to be going my way?"

"Why, I have got some business with Toney at the *Argus*," Lark said. "I'll walk that far with you."

As they went down Main Street in the direction of the courthouse, the sheriff took the inside, close to the building fronts. When Lark turned off, he chuckled as he watched the portly sheriff quicken his pace, almost running, toward the safety of his office in the jail.

Lark opened the door of the lighted *Argus* office and stepped inside. At the clangor of the bell, Thomas Toney looked up from his desk. The man's hand strayed toward a pistol lying on the desk, then seeing who his visitor was, he desisted, and relaxed visibly.

"Think you might be in for the same treatment

as your predecessor?" Lark asked.

"No reason for that, but with a killer loose, a man must take whatever precautions he can," the editor said.

"Right you are. I just had a little palaver with the sheriff, and he hasn't come up with any suspects. He says it must be someone who hates the New Eden people."

"Now that's a sage observation, when it was two of the Joshuans who were killed, and The Shepherd missed by an eyelash," Toney said sarcastically. "Slagg is a blundering—" He stopped, shaking his head. "What can I do for you?"

"Just a friendly visit, maybe ask about the Carpenter story," Lark said resting a hip on the corner of Toney's desk.

"Can't use it this issue, everybody in Hardup County wants to hear every detail about the shooting, and I'm giving them both barrels," Toney said.

"That's O.K., Mrs. Carpenter and I aren't making the progress we had hoped for anyhow. Next week will be better. Say, anything new on the gunplay?"

Toney shook his head. "The bare facts and a hundred rumors. I haven't managed to get a statement from The Shepherd. One of his men said Danville is upset, mighty upset. He plans some drastic action, but the man didn't know, or wouldn't say, what that might be."

"The Shepherd carries a pretty big stick as far as

136

Acheron is concerned, I've learned," Lark said.

"Yes, we all pretty much march to his tune," the editor said sourly. "There are a few who don't approve of his methods, but they keep their mouths shut."

"I see—the cautious course, eh? One thing really puzzles me, Toney. How does The Shepherd get away with this plural marriage he permits in New Eden? That's a federal offense now, you know."

"You know, Lark, you ask a hell of a lot of questions? But I'll answer that one. The Shepherd has friends in high places."

"And low," Lark said, drily. "I had a reason for asking. Through our Denver office of Carpenter Ranche, I got word that a U.S. marshal would soon be sent to Acheron. Can't imagine what there would be to bring a marshal here except maybe this bigamy thing. Maybe it's just a rumor."

"You don't know when?" Toney asked, seeming agitated. "The Shepherd should know this, so he can take—er, appropriate measures."

"Quite a chore to divorce six wives on short notice," Lark said. "Well, that's his problem. Guess I'll run along and hit the hay."

As he closed the outer door behind him and stepped out of the square of lamplight, he knew with satisfaction that Toney was staring after him with indecision. In the morning a horseman would take the rumor to The Shepherd. Stir things up, Lark thought, that was the Pinkerton rule. Sonya had begun it, Elnora Henty had made it boil, now he had thrown a monkey wrench into the machinery that had been running so smoothly. Let's make it worse, he thought.

Instead of turning down Main Street toward the Morris House, Lark paused at the corner in the dark. The town was quiet, almost torpid. He saw a light in the courthouse, and here and there along the street was a glow of illumination from the lamps of saloons or brothels. The night was overcast, no moon or stars to dispel the inky blackness. And quiet—from far down the street he could hear the raddled strains of honkytonk piano, but that was all. He saw no riders, no pedestrians.

He waited with that monumental patience a Pinkerton man learns. Behind him he could see the single glow of the newspaper office, the only light on the whole side street. A quarter hour passed, a half hour, without movement, without a passerby. Lark checked the Colt in his shoulder holster, and moved silent as a cat up the side street on the side opposite from the *Argus* office. There was no sidewalk here, and Lark's footsteps were soundless in the dust. Peering across at the lighted building, he could see Toney's bent head as the man worked on at the desk. Laboring, Lark thought, over his gory saga of mystery and murder.

Lark drew his revolver. Stir things up, he thought, and as fast as he could pull the trigger he slammed five shots into the newspaper office. The glass of the front window crashed. Toney's chair went over backward, and the editor disappeared behind the desk, even though Lark had been careful not to shoot close to the man.

138

The echo of the last shot had hardly died when Lark was running hard toward the corner. As he ran he broke the pistol and blew the smoke from it.

The pistol went back into the shoulder holster. Lark turned the corner and, at a more sedate pace, walked toward the hotel. It was a night even duller than usual in Acheron, and he met not a soul. The sound of gunfire had certainly been heard, but with a killer loose, no one was about to investigate the matter in the dark.

There was no clerk at the hotel desk—the interminable poker game must be going on in the back room. Upstairs, Lark locked the door of his room and lit the lamps. With a cleaning kit from his small trunk, he cleaned his pistol and reloaded it. The five empty cartridges could go into somebody's privy in the morning. Pulling off his dusty boots, he brushed them with a shoe rag. He undressed, blew out the lamps, and went to bed, pleased with the happenings of the day.

He had certainly stirred things up. Tom Toney would undoubtedly write up the "unwarranted attack on ye editor," and add to the tension in a community already jittery about shots from the dark. And he would relay to New Eden the rumor that a U.S. marshal was coming here. Lark did not know whether that was true, but he expected that sooner or later his Chicago office would manage to get Washington to order a man into the region. With Montana soon becoming a state, the powers-that-be must keep a close eye on its politics and how the new government would affect the Party.

Things were coming to a head, Lark sensed. With Sonya, and Art Rankine in the inner circles of New Eden, there would be action soon. Just what form it would take Lark did not know, but he felt he was gathering the initiative into his own hands. On this thought he sighed and dropped into the sleep of the just.

# Chapter X

Danny Henty carefully parted the tall weeds that masked the north abutment of the stone dam. Lark saw that the boy had contrived an artful viewpoint from which he could see and not be seen. Through the opening Lark had his first sight of the colony of New Eden. He was unprepared for the extent of the spread. Danville must have spent money like water—the money of the disciples, of course—for even with slave labor the many buildings must have been costly.

There were four large barns, a number of pigsties, chicken runs, and sheds. Some distance beyond Lark saw a large verandahed building which must be the community hall. Beyond that were ranks of flats which would be the home of the disciples. Off to the north were several large cottages, each surrounded by green lawn, the houses trim with new paint. Past the buildings fields opened up, some pastures holding fine-looking horses, cattle, and sheep. Others were marked by long straight rows of vegetables, with a few distant figures stooping to remove any weed which might encroach on The Shepherd's realm. The large swift ditch which led from the lake below the dam split into laterals which glistened in the sunlight as they fed the fields of produce.

"Some layout," Lark said softly to Danny. "Do you think your friend Von will be along pretty soon?"

"He ought to be," Danny said. "His assignment is to keep the weeds down along the pond and the canals, and to plug any muskrat holes in the banks. He gets the job because with this part away from the buildings anybody might take a chance and run off, but they know he won't on accounta his sisters."

"You said they have breakfast early."

"Yeah, but then they gather in the main hall and pray for a hour. Then they sing hymns for a hour. Then the Joshuans run 'em off to their chores."

The hymn singing must have concluded, for now small groups came from the communal hall and scattered out to various parts of the colony. Each group was accompanied by a black-clad Joshuan. The disciples wore white, a kind of long-skirted robe, which they kilted into their cincture for ease of movement.

Something about the scene disturbed Lark. Then it came to him. He said, "Danny, with all this—uh, marriage and so on, there should be a lot of kids around, but I don't see any."

"I been wondering about that," the boy said. "I asked Von about it, but he give me a funny look and ducked the question. There's a few boys and girls around Von's age, but I never seen any toddlers, or babes in arms."

An icy chill ran up Lark's spine. There were tribes which practiced infanticide, the Nandis of Kenya, the Western Eskimos, the Abipones of the Argentine. At one time, he remembered, the killing of babies was common in Tahiti and the Hawaiian Island. But in America, among the Indians, it had never existed as a tribal policy, even with the savage Blackfeet. But here in New Eden, were children systematically destroyed? The possibility made Lark's stomach churn at the very thought of it.

Danny raised up on his elbows. "Here comes Von now," he said.

A tall young man in a tattered white robe went into a small toolshed on the lakeshore. He came out with a hand sickle, edging it with a whetstone. With deliberation, he began cutting swaths of weeds, working toward the dam. Just below the watchers, he looked around, then called softly, "Danny, are you there?"

"I'm here, Von, and I've brought Mr. Lark with me," the boy said.

"Hello, Lavon, we're here to help you," Lark said.

Lavon Carvell was lean, almost emaciated. His hair was long and unkempt. One lens of the steel-rimmed glasses on his ascetic face was cracked.

"God knows we can use help, Mr. Lark," Lavon said. "Is Di all right?"

"She's fine. She's in Acheron moving heaven and earth to get you and the girls out of this mess," Lark told him.

"You named it, Mr. Lark. How I could be such a damned fool—well, there's no use crying about it now. But I hope you move fast, sir. Things are getting worse. Elihu Noon—" The young man shook his head.

"We'll do our best," Lark assured him. "Lavon, were you able to get through to the Countess Verloff?"

"Yes, through my sister Kris. Kris gave me a note from the Countess."

Lark unfolded the paper and scanned it quickly:

"Ah, what a sweet new Eden! Fifty holy disciples, and twenty dedicated Joshuans. Our Shepherd Joshua, and his evangelist, Elihu. My sins are washed away in the blood of the Lamb. I have forsworn the lusts of the flesh, for though The Shepherd says kindred souls should marry and meld, I feel as yet there is no balm in Gilead. My duty is to convert the weak ones to our sweet beliefs, notably the sinner Flaherty whom I try to win over every day. I pray for a sign from heaven, for The Shepherd urges me to give my all soon. With fear and trembling I await word from the angel, for the devils rattle their tridents, and will soon erase all sin from a worldly Hell."

What a woman! Lark thought, a wave of admiration and love and longing sweeping over him so intense that he had to swallow and turn away for a moment. Even the most suspicious Joshuan would not have suspected a message in Sonya's note if it had been intercepted.

He said, "Lavon, have your sister pass the word to the Countess that we got her note, and will keep

144

in touch. And we hope to move within the week. She is to be careful, very careful. You can trust the Countess, Lavon, and the man Flaherty, too. They are our people."

They talked a while longer, with Carvell taking an occasional cut with his sharp sickle to appear busy. Now in the distance a horseman turned this way. Lavon saw the man.

He said hurriedly, "It's been great talking to you, Mr. Lark. Except for Danny I've felt so alone. Now you better duck. Here comes the Siskiyou Kid, the irrigation foreman."

Danny Henty and Lark slid down so they were in concealment, but could still watch. The horseman tied his mount by the toolshed and came on foot, to the foot of the dam where Lavon was working.

The Siskiyou Kid was tall and skinny, tipped to the side by the weight of the forty-five on his gunbelt. As the man approached, Lavon stopped cutting and stood in an attitude of humility, his head bowed. The Joshuan reached out and jerked Lavon's chin up with a fist.

"You pup, you call this working?" he rasped. "These weeds grow faster than you move. You better come to time or we'll take your elixir away from you."

"Oh, don't do that!" Lavon pleaded. "I was working slowly because I don't feel so good this morning."

"Some excuse! You'll really feel bad when I get through with you!" Siskiyou said. He smashed a fist to the side of the boy's face and Lavon went down. He lay there, looking up at the Kid like a hurt dog.

Lark's temper flared. Crazy saddle tramp, he thought, gets fun out of hurting things. Beside him, Lark felt Danny gather himself. "Not now, kid," he whispered, a restraining hand on the boy's back. "Not now."

When Lavon came slowly to his feet, the Kid knocked him down again. He said, "Sonny, you got to learn your place. You can't get smart with me, even if you are soon gonna be my brother-in-law."

Lavon came to hands and knees, staring up. He asked, "Wh—what do you mean?"

"Why, The Shepherd don't hone to screw none of this young stuff when he's getting a seasoned beauty like the Countess. He's turning your sisters over to me'n Fat Tex." He stood over Carvell, laughing, his feet spread.

With a wordless cry, Lavon surged to his feet. He swung the sickle he was holding in a furious arc. The keen edge caught the saddle tramp on his long skinny neck and crunched through flesh and bone. The head of the Siskiyou Kid leaped clear of his trunk. It rolled down the slope like a bowling ball. Strangely, for a long moment the headless torso stood erect, blood gouting from the severed arteries. Then like a broken puppet it collapsed and slumped down, to lie without motion.

"Good God!" Lark exclaimed, and without regard for circumstance, came down from his concealment. He put an arm about Lavon's shoulders, for the boy was paralyzed by what he

146

had done, and was about to fall.

"It's all right, Von, it's all right," he said. "He had it coming. But this tears the rag off the bush. You've got to come with us, right now, or the Joshuans will tear you into little pieces."

The boy drew a deep shuddering breath and averted his eyes from the headless corpse. Then his jaw set and he looked at Lark. "I can't, Mr. Lark. I can't abandon my sisters. I'll take my chances."

Lark rubbed his jaw, thinking. "Well, since you're mule-stubborn, maybe there's another way. It'll be hell to explain a body without a head, so we've got to get rid of it. You and Danny go up to the toolshed and unsaddle the Kid's horse, put the tack in the tool shed. Then chase the horse away. Any burlap sacks in the shed? Bring two or three. And a shovel."

While the boys were gone he washed the bloody sickle in the running ditch. He saw the Kid's horse, without saddle and bridle, trotting away toward the barns. The boys came back with sacks and shovel, looking less pale and wan than they had before. Boys are resilient, thank God, Lark thought.

He managed the gruesome task of putting the severed head into a sack, and was glad when the staring eyes of the Siskiyou Kid were hidden. He covered the neck of the trunk with other bags, and tied them securely under the arms of the corpse. He washed his hands in the canal, then shoveled the sodden earth into the running water until no trace remained. He washed the shovel and gave it to Lavon. "Put the shovel and sickle in the shed,

Von, and shut the door," he said. "Now here's your story—tell it the same every time they ask you, and stick to it. The Siskiyou Kid rode down here, talked to you, and rode away. You never saw him again. You went up to the hall when the bell rang for noon prayers. The Kid didn't come back to the dam. Now don't embroider it, tell it flat and straight. If you hang tough, you're all right."

"Thanks, Mr. Lark, I think I can do it. But what about that?" He motioned toward the corpse.

"We'll take care of that," Lark said. "Now remember, son, don't go around looking like a dying duck in a thunderstorm. You did what you had to do and you can be proud of it. If things get too bad, turn to the Countess and Frank Flaherty."

At that moment a distant bell began to clang, the New Eden parody of the Angelus. Lavon Carvell grinned, waved a hand, and started toward the main hall at a high lope. Lark took one last look around, nodded, and stooping, picked up the body of the Siskiyou Kid and slung it over his shoulder. He jerked a thumb at the gunnysack. Danny gulped, then with averted head, picked it up. The two made their way with their burdens up the abutment of the dam and over the far side. "Move it, Danny," Lark said. "We've got to get rid of this reprobate fast, before the Joshuans miss him."

The trip was uneventful, and they made good time over Danny's secret route. Lark breathed a sigh of relief when at last they ducked under the four strands of barbed wire, for though skinny and headless, the Siskiyou Kid had grown tarnation heavy by the end of the second mile.

Off New Eden land, while the two rested Lark asked, "Got any ideas on where to stash this fellow?"

"Wisht we'd brung that shovel, but we didn't. Say there's a steep cutbank about a quarter mile west of here. The shale and clay are sloughing. Mebbe we could cave some more down and cover him up."

"Better than leaving him for the coyotes," Lark said. He shouldered his burden. "All right, let's go."

At the bottom of the cliff they found a pile of loose material against the face of the bank. With bare hands the two scrabbled a shallow hollow in it, and Lark laid the body of the Siskiyou Kid in it. With obvious relief Danny added the sack with the head, Lark tossed in the man's pistol. He said, "I'm going to see if I can cave down some of the bank to cover him, Danny."

The slope was nearly sheer, but Lark managed to scramble up some twenty feet to a narrow ledge. He kicked at the edge until he loosened a small slide, then another. He clung to an indentation and peered down. It helps some, he thought, but we need a wagonload.

At that moment the earth gave way beneath his feet. He began to slide, scratching at the wall with frantic fingers. Halfway down he caught at a spindly bush, which slowed him a little before its roots gave way. Lark landed at the bottom with a spine-tingling jar, scratched and bleeding and out of breath.

"Are you O.K., Mr. Lark?" Danny asked anxiously.

Lark brushed the clay from his clothes. "Guess so, son. I didn't intend to come down quite that fast, and that's a gut."

Danny, free of his grisly burden, was himself again. He grinned and said, "Well, you sure done what you meant to do, Mr. Lark. The Siskiyou Kid is safe under twenty feet of dirt and rock."

Lark checked the sizable pile of detritus. "May he sleep well, the hound. Yes, he'll be protected from coyotes until this affair is over. Then we can dig him out, put him together, and give him a proper ceremony."

"He don't deserve no better than this cutbank," Danny said. "Say, Mr. Lark, did you ever see such a turrible blow as Von swung with his sickle?"

"What he did couldn't be duplicated," Lark agreed. "The threat to his sisters made him explode. But we must forget Von's part in what we saw, son. Someone might call it murder, and make trouble for the young man. Best keep it under our hats forever."

"I'll never breathe a word, Mr. Lark, and you can count on it," Danny said. He caught sight of a black stain on his hand, and scrubbed it furiously with a handful of dirt. "I just as soon never seen it. They way the head bounced toward the ditch, all by itself . . ."

"Well, son, there's one less Joshuan to deal with, and that's a bonus," Lark said, putting a hand on the boy's shoulder. "Come on, let's go."

They were almost to the pond when Danny gasped, "Oh, God, Mr. Lark, Von's white robe!"

"Forget it, kid. I checked before he left. There wasn't a spot of blood on it," Lark told him, and Danny breathed again.

Mrs. Henty and Diane were seated on the porch of the Circle H ranchhouse behind the trellis of wild cucumber vines. The Spencer leaned conveniently against the house wall. Diane came to her feet as Lark and the boy came up. "How is Von?" she cried. "Are our girls all right? And Sonya?"

"Hold your horses, lady, all in due time," Lark said, sitting down on the edge of the porch and sifting Bull Durham into a Riz la Croix brown paper. When the quirly was built and lit to his satisfaction, he said, "Yes, we saw Von, and he is O.K. for the moment. And The Shepherd has changed his plan about the girls. He is concentrating on the Countess instead. She passed us a note—everyone seems more afraid of Elihu Noon than The Shepherd. And there may be reprisals against Acheron."

Mrs. Henty pursed her lips. "They'll hurt innocent people. I've got to go to town and turn myself in to Sheriff Slagg. It don't matter about me, I'll confess and mebbe keep others from getting hurt."

"No, no, Mrs. Henty," Lark said. "That would really turn loose the dogs of war. You keep lying low, we'll handle it. Sonya tells me there are some fifty disciples, and twenty Joshuans. One of those men is mine. Maybe between him and Sonya we can stiffen the spines of some of the disciples to give us a hand when the showdown comes."

"I wouldn't count on them, Mr. Lark. I didn't tell you before, but Von told me the disciples get something in their coffee. It makes 'em kinda dull and quiet, like—like dolls. Von got wise and quit taking coffee, and warned his sisters."

"Some hypnotic drug," Lark said. "No wonder the people are easy to handle. Danny, don't go in by the secret trail tomorrow. Let things—er, cool off a bit, eh? Wait until you get word from me."

"I gotcha, Mr. Lark," Danny said, grinning. "Anyhow, I have chores to do, I'm behind on 'em. Gee, I wish Von had known somethin' about my ma."

"With Marshall gone, she'll be all right," Diane said. "We'll soon have them all out of there. I have Justin Lark's promise."

Riding back to Acheron, Lark reluctantly told Diane his theory about the missing children. He did not relish adding to the girl's worries, but thought she should know his suspicions. Then added, "This thing is coming to a head, like a carbuncle that must be lanced. And we're going to lance it. I have some more men coming, Diane. I've planted some nasty rumors that will shake up the Joshuans. But this business of reprisals worries me. If they move before we are ready, it means Kate Muldoon and Racklin and Warner, among others are in deadly danger."

"And Sonya, your wife—if they find she's an impostor they'll do something terrible."

"If anyone harms my darling, I'll take the whole

place apart," Lark said grimly. "If I have to do it singlehanded. I'm banking on her courage and coolness, she has been in tight spots before this one."

"I pray no harm comes to her, or the girls, or Von," Diane said.

"And we must save those poor, drugged, misguided disciples from The Shepherd and Elihu Noon and the rest," Lark said. "Lady, this has become more than a Pinkerton case to me. I'm going to destroy this sweet deadly Eden, if it's the last thing I do."

"Which might be, if our luck is bad," Diane said soberly.

## Chapter XI

The saddle tramp who stopped Lark on Main Street was lean, grizzled, and obviously down on his luck. He said, "Stranger, I'm sorta ridin' the chuck line. I've already et my saddle and my spurs are in Uncle's window. You look like a prosperous and kindhearted soul. How's for a grubstake to keep a poor cowboy's body and spirit together?"

Taking out his wallet, Lark gave the man a double eagle. "Take this," he said. "Two blocks down, there's a boarding house, Mrs. Gaspar's. Hole up there until you catch onto a job. If I hear of anybody that needs a cowpoke, I'll pass on the word."

"God bless you, mister," the rider said, reaching out a callused hand. "My moniker is Val—Val Kleberg, out of Ft. Benton, which place I wisht to hell I never left."

"Justin Lark, Kleberg," Lark said, shaking hands. "I'm at the Morris House. Let me know if you have a change of luck."

Lark was smiling as the man went off down the street. Val Kleberg was one of the top operatives out of the Denver office. He had been one of the crew that broke up the vicious Redtop gang at Stoneman's Gap. So Eames must have the others coming to Acheron.

Lark was sitting in his room, rocking gently, his hands behind his head. He was enjoying the cool breeze that ruffled the window curtains, and trying to quell the impatience that rose in him. He could sense, from long experience, that this case was coming to a climax. It was hard to be calm in the face of coming action, yet the waiting seemed to take forever.

He stood up at a soft coded rap at the door, smiling. Yet he was not prepared for the two men who stood in the hall. "Come on, get in here, you two rogues!" he exclaimed. "I don't want you seen with me."

Inside, Con Tetrault gave Lark a bear hug. Then Bill Collins clamped on a handshake that crunched Lark's bones. Tetrault appropriated the rocker, and Collins helped himself to a cigarette from the box of Sweet Caporals on the dresser. He lit it and sat on the edge of the bed. "Coming up in the world, smoking tailormades, eh? Easy to tell you're on the ol' expense account."

"Those are for town, I still smoke quirlies out on the range," Lark said, grinning. "A man who has to live in this fleabag needs a few creature comforts. Con, you old faker, you just couldn't stay away from the action, eh? How's our sweet Rimi, and the twins?"

"Great. She sends her love to you. The Gap's so busy with the railroad surveyors and engineers and

155

all, I wanted to turn Sam Eames down, but Rimi insisted that I give you a hand. I think she wants me to keep you from getting hurt, because she's still in love with you."

"And I am with her. But I'm glad to have you, you old goat, and you too, Bill. How did you happen to get on this case?"

"I'd just wound up an embezzlement case in Spokane," Collins said. "I got Sam's wire and hopped the varnish for Acheron. Got a surprise when I ran across Con on the train."

"How was your Spokane case? Tough?"

Collins shook his head. "Run of the mill. A bank teller playing the horses and the women, picking away at inactive accounts. I picked up his trail the second day. The guy pegged me and the next night he cleaned out the vault. But I had a line on his lady friend, so when they came to the train steps I was waiting. The guy had twenty thou in his keister, now he has twenty years in Walla Walla."

"You make it sound so simple," Lark said drily. "Well, for this New Eden case you'll need one hell of a lot more nerve and finesse. Looks as if we're in for some hard riding and hot lead. There's a passel of tough rannies on t'other side, as Val Kleberg might say. By the way, Val's already in town."

As briefly as he could he outlined the Carvell story, what he and Diane and Danny Henty had learned, the shooting at the depot, and the threat of reprisals against Acheron citizens.

"The sheriff and the county attorney are crooked. I've asked Chicago for a couple of U.S.

marshals, but I don't know if or when they are coming. It's one nasty, dangerous mess, boys, but we've got to bust it wide open, and get those poor Carvell kids and the others out of it. And keep this cancer from spreading to the whole of Montana."

"Have we got anyone on the inside?" Tetrault asked.

"Yes. One of the Joshuans is Art Rankine, posing as Frank Flaherty, the ex-marshal of Magma. And a rich widow, becoming a convert— the Countess Verloff."

"Sonya? Good God, Justin, how could you let Eames tangle that lovely lady of yours up in an explosive case like this one?" Tetrault rasped.

"I didn't have a damned thing to say about it, and I doubt if Sam had much. Sonya wanted a piece of the action, and you know Sonya. The word is she has The Shepherd eating out of her hand, and she's keeping us in touch through the boy Danny Henty."

"Have you figured out a plan, Justin?" Bill Collins asked.

"Yes, but it's pretty half-assed. Can't do much until we have all our crew. You guys get together with Val Kleberg, rent some horses. Keep an eye on Sheriff Slagg, and Tom Toney, the editor of the paper. Hang around the Silver Dollar saloon. Damn! I wish the initiative was ours now, but it isn't. We'll have to wait for the Joshuans' next move, and hope that Sonya and Art get word to us in time to copper it."

"I'd say that a raid, a pitched battle, is the last thing we want," Collins said. "We're trying to save those poor souls in New Eden, not get them massacred. Seems to me our best bet is this Shepherd, Danville."

"Kidnap him?" Tetrault asked.

Lark smiled. "My God, you boys have devious minds. Yes, the idea had occurred to me, but the man is always well guarded by a bunch of very hard hardcases. If we could work some kind of trap . . ."

"Guess we'll have to play it by ear, as the man with the tin whistle said," Con Tetrault said.

"Let's get together tomorrow night," Lark said. "I'm sending the boy Danny in to see if he can pick up a message from Sonya or Art. Our other boys should be here, too. I'll have Shank Morris, the hotel man, set up a table in here for a friendly poker game, some beer, cheese and crackers, and so on. We'll turn it into a council of war."

The next morning, walking back from breakfast at Kate Muldoon's, Lark said to Diane, "Dammit, lady, I don't like this, sending you off to Circle H alone. But with men coming and the Joshuans all stirred up, I can't leave. Now you listen—just give Danny my instructions, send him off, and wait with Mrs. Henty for the kid to return. Don't you go off on some hare-brained tangent of your own, you hear me?"

"I'll be a good girl," Diane said demurely. "Since Ellie Henty has her Spencer back, I'll take along my own rifle—in case of coyotes, you know."

"See that you behave. I've got enough to worry about already."

"You're not half as worried as I am, Justin," she said, her lips taut. "We must come to the end of it soon, or I'll fly into little splinters."

He helped Diane saddle Barnaby and saw her off to the Henty ranch. Then he walked to the depot, for the westbound train, No. 25, was due shortly. He was hoping additional men would be on it, perhaps the U.S. marshals. The badly needed men must come soon, or he would have to move without them.

Standing in a patch of thin shade, Lark watched the passengers get off. A banker type, in black broadcloth, string tie, and a derby; a rancher in Stetson, high-heeled boots, carrying a canvas valise; a small man with a harsh ascetic face, wearing a business suit and a cream Panama. The rancher stopped beside Lark.

"Say, bud, is there a decent hotel in this burg?" he asked.

"The Morris House is passable," Lark said. "A couple blocks down the street," he said pointing.

"Thanks, pardner," the man said.

Lark muttered softly, "Room twenty-two. Seven o'clock."

The rancher paid no attention. He caught up with the banker type and the two crossed the street and went on toward the hotel.

Lark watched them, pleased. Marley Belote and Jubal Harnish were top Pinkerton operatives. Trust them not to tip their hands, he thought. Things are beginning to shape up.

The small man picked up his valise and came toward Lark. Sensing an intentness, Lark waited.

159

The man stopped, took a slip of paper from his pocket, looked at it, looked at Lark. His eyes were gray and cold.

"Are you Justin Lark?" he asked.

Lark's right hand crept to the left lapel of his jacket. "I am," he said.

"I'm United States Marshal Adam Beckett. I've been ordered here from Miles City to handle a problem. You are to give me information." There was no friendliness in Beckett's voice.

"May I see your credentials?" Lark asked.

Beckett opened his coat to show a badge, and handed Lark a letter. It bore an ornate gold seal and a signature Lark recognized. Lark was to provide every assistance to Marshal Adam Beckett of the Montana District.

"You'll want a room," Lark said. "The Morris House is O.K. When you've registered, I'll come into the lobby and we'll talk in private. No eavesdroppers to contend with there. In Acheron even the walls have ears, as Cervantes says."

"Well, an educated son-of-a-bitch!" Beckett said coldly. He picked up his valise again and strode away without another word.

Lark stared after him. I don't like this little bastard, he thought. I'm going to have trouble with him before we're through.

He delayed for a few minutes, then followed Beckett into the lobby of the Morris House. He found a saloon chair on the far side of the lobby, and picked up the *Argus*. He grinned as he read Tom Toney's lurid account of the dastardly night attack on Ye Editor. A boxed editorial called for strong action from the sheriff, the Territory of Montana, and the Federal Government, not leaving out the U.S. Army. "This killer must be brought to justice, and a deserved fate on the gallows." Good going, Tom, Lark approved. That will stir things up some more.

Beckett came down the stairs and joined Lark at the lobby table. To Lark's amazement, the marshal was wearing his badge of office openly. He said, "You want your presence in Acheron known, Beckett?"

"Of course," the marshal said. "I represent the majesty of the United States of America. Just my being here will make the evildoers think twice. I'm in charge of this New Eden case now, y'understand. So I'll have it cleaned up before the week is out."

Lark watched Beckett take out a cigar case, select a stogie, clip the end, and light it with great care. He did not offer the case to Lark. Lark took one of his Sweet Caporals from its box, flicked a kitchen match into light with a thumbnail, and lit the cigarette. He leaned back, blue smoke dribbling from his nostrils, waiting for the little man to go on.

He had met a number of federal marshals on his various cases. Most had been dedicated men, handling their dull or dangerous tasks with courage, brains, and ability. But a few had been political appointees, who had known someone in high places, or paid off for a political debt. These had proven both incompetent and dangerous, puffed with the importance of their office, bumbling around immune to advice. Lark pegged Adam Beckett as one of the latter, a man to be handled with great caution.

"How do you suggest we proceed?" Lark asked.

"First, let me say I have concluded from the data I have that this case is a matter of the separation of church and state, as provided in the U.S. Constitution. In my opinion the Pinkerton Agency and others are harassing the Reverend Hiram Danville in a matter of religion, involving the New Eden sect at their colony."

"Oh, come off it, Beckett! Danville's New Eden is a prison for the poor disciples who have mistakenly given their money to Danville and are now slaves. The man uses every kind of coercion—drugs, gunmen, hypnotism—to keep these poor souls from liberty."

"You haven't proved any of that," Beckett said. "And just what is your stake in the attempt to destroy this New Eden?"

"I have a client whose relatives are being held against their will in New Eden, after paying The Shepherd, Danville, some very large sums of money. The security at the colony is so tight we haven't even been able to hear from my client's people."

"So you're biased, Lark? I think I'd better get to the bottom of this in my own way. I'll talk to the local sheriff and the county attorney. Perhaps to some private citizens, and of course to the Reverend Danville. Meantime, I don't want you taking further action without my approval."

There was no use arguing, Lark saw. "The

162

sheriff and the county attorney have offices in the courthouse, the stone building at the end of the street. One thing, marshal—my connection with Pinkerton's is not known in Acheron. I'm sure our Chicago office would be very, very unhappy if by accident or design you blew my cover. They do have important connections in Washington, you know."

Beckett stared at Lark, then nodded. "I'm an experienced lawman, Lark. I will assure you of my discretion. Unless of course it becomes necessary to reveal your motives." The marshal tossed the stub of his cigar hissing into the cuspidor and stood up. "If anything comes up that I should know for my investigation, let me know immediately."

Watching Beckett walk cockily across the lobby and out the hotel door, Lark shook his head. As my daddy always said, conceit is God's gift to the little man, he thought. That guy should be serving court papers or inspecting cattle shipments. Either he'll take the train out of here with nothing done, or he will come head to head with The Shepherd and his Joshuans and there will be hell to pay. I can't use him, I've got to go ahead with my own plans without the "majesty of the U.S. Government."

From the time he parted from the marshal, the day dragged unbearably for Lark. He was used to action, used to being in the driver's seat. With frustration boiling in him, he ate lunch at Kate Muldoon's. He told her, "My men are all here, Kate. We'll move soon. And a U.S. marshal arrived, a man named Beckett. I don't think he will be of any help to us, he's not the type. So if he tries to pump you, clam up. He may try to use some harum-scarum methods on New Eden. That won't work, and some people will get hurt. I can't have that."

"Of course not. I'll be discreet if Beckett approaches me. Justin, Diane told me what you suspect about the children. What a horrible thing! But it could be possible. Thinking back, I can never remember seeing a New Eden child, and there's no school there."

"Suspicion without evidence, I admit, but the possibility makes me purely sick," Lark said. "Damn! I wish that girl would get back."

"Justin, it's only noon," Kate chided.

That night anyone going down the hall past Room 22 would have heard the click of poker chips, a hum of voices, and an occasional laugh. But the six men in the room were playing for higher stakes than money, stakes of life and death.

Con Tetrault riffled a deck of cards. He said, "I agree, Justin. This Beckett is dam' likely to throw a sprag in the wheels of progress."

"I didn't spill anything to the little guy, except that Pinkerton's was trying to get some clients out of New Eden," Lark said. "He antagonized me the minute I met him, and I didn't trust him."

"Think he'll get anything out of Sheriff Slagg?" Tetrault asked.

Lark shook his head. "Not even the right time of day. Slagg is as crooked as a kid's jump rope. Beckett will make Danville nervous, though. I planted a rumor that a marshal was coming, now

Slagg will get word to The Shepherd that the man is here in Acheron."

There was a soft tap at the door. Lark opened the door to find Diane Carvell, still in riding clothes. She came in and he shut the door. She seemed to be surprised at so many men. He introduced her around. Smiling, she said, "A small army to take on a score of Joshuans."

"We're rough and tough and hard to curry, Miss Carvell," Bill Collins said.

"You'll have to be," she said, frowning. She handed Lark some papers. "I thought a written report would be best. And there's a letter from your wife. Justin, I've got to go now, to keep Kate Muldoon company."

"Do that, Diane, since you've got it all down here in black and white. I'll see you at breakfast and bring you up to date."

Lark saw Bill Collins staring admiringly at Diane as the girl went out. "Too bad she was in such a hurry," Collins said. "I'd like to know her better—a lot better."

"Don't blame you, she's got a couple million dollars stashed in the bank," Lark said. "Besides being damned pretty. As for her hurry, she had a good reason, to get shut of me in a hurry before I skinned her alive. Boys, she took these notes herself. The little idiot went to New Eden with Danny, after I had ordered her absolutely not to do that." He shook his head in despair. "Women, women."

"As an old married man, you must have learned the lesson I did," Tetrault said, grinning.

"Women act as they please, not as they are told. What does Diane have to say?"

"Von told her New Eden has been buzzing. One of the Joshuans has disappeared without a trace, the Siskiyou Kid. Then Tom Toney, the editor, came riding out yesterday and the rumor went around that there was a U.S. marshal coming to investigate the colony. Of course Lavon had a tearful reunion with Diane. She told him it was brave of him to stay for the sake of Kristin and Gracia, his sisters. And to keep up his role of messenger with Danny, it was important. We would soon have a showdown with the Shepherd and have all the disciples out of the colony."

"Good. And what does Sonya say?" Tetrault asked.

"I'll read it to you," Lark said. This time his wife hadn't disguised her message with religious cant. It read:

> First and most important, Justin, if you love me as I love you, get me out of this madhouse quickly. I have managed to elude The Shepherd so far, though he is very persistent and also most horny, as our cowboys used to say. He threatens if I do not submit he will make the Carvell girls wives of his, No. 7 and No. 8. That, he says will bring me to my senses. I am still what you call stalling him, for a little more, though I am not afraid of this tomcat Danville. It is his assistant, Elihu Noon, we all fear and despise. I think the man

*is a lunatic.*

*Noon is furious at the news a government man is snooping in Acheron. He says the Great Jehovah will strike down that man and all others who threaten New Eden and the life beyond, which is even better.*

*Maybe that is why The Shepherd and half his men are riding into town tomorrow. Art Rankine got word to me that he will be in the escort. Noon is convinced that the town has gone too long unpunished for the deaths of Blackie Legrand and Monte Marshall, and there is the matter of the U.S. marshal. Noon says the town needs a lesson, so The Shepherd leaves tomorrow at ten o'clock. I saw some men taking target practice down by the barns. When the Joshuans come, Justin, darling, be very very careful, for I love you.*

*Your own Sonya.*

"I wonder what kind of lesson Danville intends," Kleberg said, frowning. "I thought the whole town was on his side. One thing, notice that he is splitting his forces. If we have to take 'em on, half is better than the whole army."

"Most of the town and the officials are under The Shepherd's thumb," Lark said. "But there are a few dissidents, and I don't doubt Danville knows who they are. Even if he punishes a wrong person or two, he won't care. He has delusions of grandeur, a Napoleon on horseback."

"There's going to be blood on the moon,"

Kleberg said. "Justin, this town of Acheron is about as crummy a spread as I ever saw, but we can't let a massacre happen. We've got to stop it."

"You're right, Val. Since we don't know just what Danville intends, let's play our cards this way . . ."

When his men left, each with his assignment for the next day, Lark was not a happy man. He had made preparations as best he could, but he hated to leave the initiative with Danville. He didn't know what Sheriff Slagg would do. Adam Beckett was an unknown quantity, while his presence made it impossible for Lark and his men to take the role of aggressors. Finally he shrugged, and left it, as Sonya would say, in the lap of the gods.

At a rap on his door, he let Diane in. He looked at her sternly, then he put his hands on her shoulders and shook her. "You spoiled brat, don't you know what you did today was dangerous?" he demanded. "You could have gotten yourself and Danny killed, maybe Von, too."

"I know, Justin," she said humbly. "We nearly did get caught on the way back, by a patrol of Joshuans. I think they were looking for the missing man, the Siskiyou Kid. Danny found us a hidey-hole just in time. I was scared, Justin, of the Joshuans and of rattlesnakes."

"I hope you learned your lesson, young lady," he said grumpily. "Now here's your assignment for tomorrow—when we go to breakfast, take your rifle and cartridges. You'll stay with Kate. I think she might be one of The Shepherd's targets."

"Oh, not Kate!" Diane cried. "I'll do it, Justin.

168

If any of those men try to get at her, I'll shoot them dead."

"Good girl. I hope it won't come to that, but it might. How was Von?"

"Oh, the poor boy was so thin and pale and frightened. But it was wonderful to see him, to talk with him. Justin, I'm afraid for the boy. He says he's suspected of something, he didn't say what."

"Everyone out there is in danger, Diane. We've got to get this thing over with," he said. The disciples, he thought, the Carvells, but most of all Sonya. If anything happened to her . . .

Diane sensed his concern. She pressed soft lips to his cheek. "She'll be all right, Justin," she said. "I'm sure she will."

## Chapter XII

Returning from breakfast without Diane, Lark found his room already made up, for this was the day the Morris House furnished clean sheets. Lark let the window shades fly up and stood looking out at Main Street.

Towns are like live things, he thought, I've sensed their temper before this. Acheron has been dull with fright, unfriendly, suspicious. It smelled of treachery. But today there was motion in the town, a sense of something impending, something exciting, perhaps deadly. What mystic grapevine, what eerie electricity, is flowing through Acheron to give the town this air of premonition? I wonder if Tombstone felt like this on the day of the corral fight eight years ago.

He took the Winchester from the closet, tried the action, polished the stock and barrel. He had burned a box of .45-90 shells out at the Henty ranch and found the gun a joy to use, marvelously accurate and hard-hitting. He thumbed cartridges into the magazine, put on the safety, and laid the rifle on the table. He did not need to check his Colt Lightning, for it was a ritual with him to keep the pistol clean, loaded and ready.

If violence comes as retribution by the Joshuans, it will be here, in the very center of town. Otherwise the lesson might not be sufficiently impressed on the citizenry. They might not be completely convinced of the absolute mastery of The Shepherd and his men. So it must be here. And from the two windows of Room 22 Lark's men would have the whole performance under their guns, and death at their fingertips.

He was still wondering what action the sheriff would take, then remembering how Slagg had sought his company that dark night, he smiled sourly. Yet Lark hated unknown factors. Factors such as the whereabouts of Marshal Adam Beckett, and why the fanatic Noon had not come to see 'justice'''. And how the town seemed to know conflict was in the air, perhaps death. A leak from Sheriff Slagg's office, he suspected. The leaden overcast of the morning sky added to the sense of foreboding.

There was unusual activity along Main Street, at the depot, in the shops and businesses along the street. From the side window he could see the warehouses, shacks and wagon yards beyond the tracks, and the buildings of Acheron's redlight district. Though more wagons, buggies and saddlehorses were in sight than usual, Lark saw few women, and those he did see seemed to be in a hurry. Small boys were playing, walking the hitch rails, falling off, searching under the wooden sidewalks for lost coins, splashing each other with stale green water from the public watering trough. Men would gather in small clumps, disperse, regroup. He watched a mule train plod along the street and turn the corner toward the wagon yard, the skinner's blacksnake popping like gunshots, his curses searing the quiet air.

Lark had both windows opened wide. Now he pinned back the curtains, let the shades roll to the top. He saw the gaze of the men on the street turn toward the courthouse. Into sight swept a crowd of horsemen lifting the powder dust into a drifting saffron cloud. They slowed and stopped squarely in front of the Morris House. The Joshuans in sombre black, their horses sleek with sweat. They ringed The Shepherd on his magnificent black horse. Now all swung down except Hiram Danville and one of his men.

He commands good discipline, Lark thought wryly, not one of those scoundrels broke for a saloon. He's quite a dude, that Shepherd—black clothes, black boots, gunbelt and holster chased with gleaming silver, silver buttons, the hair and beard of an Old Testament prophet flowing from under the black Stetson. The horse, too, was impressive, silver mounted saddle and tack, silver conchas gleaming.

Like iron filings to a magnet, the people of Acheron moved to surround Danville and his men. The Shepherd waited—until the exact moment suited him. Then he stood in his stirrups. His voice rang out, mellow, euphonious, compelling.

"People of Acheron! My people, for soon you will see the light and join me in Eden. My prayers will be answered fully, for you will join my flock. I am The Shepherd."

In the crowd that was still gathering, Lark now saw a few women. The adults tried to chase the boys away, which was like trying to corral a flea in a teacup, though the youngsters did retreat to the fringes of the crowd.

In the odd silence, The Shepherd's voice rang out again. "You are good people worthy of my New Eden. But there are a few among you who are vipers. Vipers and liars and murderers. They have slain my loyal followers in cold blood. They have tried to murder me, The Shepherd. Now I have had a dream. In my dream an angel came to me . . ." The Shepherd bowed his head reverently, ". . . and the angel told me who those men are. 'You must scotch them,' the angel said 'as you would a rattlesnake. You must smite them hip and thigh. They must learn that The Shepherd and his cohorts of New Eden are sacrosanct, that no man's hand must be raised against them ever again.' 'When?' I asked the angel. 'Do not let tomorrow's sun go down until you have the vengeance of the Lord upon them.' At that the angel vanished with a great roar of wind, and I awoke in a cold sweat. So I have come with my anointed followers to carry out the orders of the angel."

"But Shepherd, who are these men?" a voice came from the rear of the crowd.

"As it is proclaimed in the Good Book 'He who is not with me is against me.' The traitors know me, and I know them. If they have not fled they are doomed. As Joshua led his people of old, so I lead you. So I say—I cry aloud, 'Let vengeance fall upon these heathens.' Forward men."

At last, Lark thought. He jacked a shell into the action of the rifle. He watched as two men went toward the gunsmith's, two more toward the harness shop, two more turned the corner of the side street. Two others shoved through the crowd, coming toward the hotel entrance. One of those was Art Rankine. Danville and one mounted man remained in the street, with the crowd knotted around them.

Lark heard heavy steps on the stairs. A fist pounded on the door of the room. "Open up, Justin Lark! We know you're in there!" a man shouted.

Lark put the rifle on the table and opened the door. A man shoved a pistol barrel in Lark's middle, a man he did not know, hard of feature, mean of eye. He's done time in the pen, Lark thought, he has that look about him.

"Wh-what d'you want with me?" Lark asked, trying to make his voice quaver. Over the man's shoulder, Lark caught Rankine's wink.

"The Shepherd said to bring you in," the man said. "Vigilante court is in session. We will try you for high crimes against New Eden and the sons of Joshua. Move, or we'll let you have it right here."

"All right, all right, I'm coming," Lark said, shrugging into his jacket, the better to conceal the bulge of the shoulder holster under his vest.

"What the hell's the matter with you, Cory?" Rankine asked. "Keep your gun on him." Ex-

174

pertly he ran his hands down Lark's body, armpits, legs. "He's clean, but you couldda got yourself killed."

"By this gutless bastard? Who you kidding, Frank?" He jabbed Lark with the pistol barrel. "Come on, you, move."

As the three went toward the stairs, Lark saw the door of Tetrault's room was open a crack. He knew that before he reached the lobby with his captors Con and Bill Collins would be in Room 22 ready for action.

In the street he stood between the man Cory and Art Rankine and looked up at Danville. "What is the meaning of this outrage?" he demanded. "What do you want with me?"

"Why, to hang you," The Shepherd said pleasantly. "You are a spy and a traitor, and you have consorted with known traitors. You must go, you and the others."

"What others?" Lark asked.

"Racklin, and Warner. Spivey the stableman, Osweiler the telegrapher. Some more perhaps. All have raised their hands against me, The Shepherd, and the New Eden."

"Danville, if you harm any women, if you harm Mrs. Carpenter, you'll pay for it!" Lark shouted.

The Shepherd smiled thinly through the mat of beard. "Mrs. Carpenter and the Muldoon woman will be taken care of, though they do not deserve our compassion. As to you, Justin Lark, your crimes are black as ebony. You are mixed up with those spawns of Satan, the Pinkerton Agency."

That little skunk Beckett—he did spill his guts

after all, Lark thought savagely. Wonder where the bastard is now.

Looking past Danville, he called, "Sheriff Slagg! You're the law. You can't let these maniacs hang me, an innocent man. It would be cold-blooded murder!"

The sheriff was horribly uncomfortable, forced to move into the open, to admit his allegiance in front of all these constituents. His jowls quivered, and he licked dry lips. "Cain't do much about it, Lark. You can see me and my two depitties are outgunned. We'd just get ourselves killed, too."

"Slagg, you're a damned lily-livered coward!" Lark growled. "All right, Danville, as long as you have the guns and your minds are made up, let's get on with it."

"When we're ready, after the other candidates are sworn in," The Shepherd said, pink lips twisting. "Don't be so anxious to travel the road to meet your maker, Lark. Possess yourself in patience."

The crowd milled uncertainly, the excitement dying, the gravity of what was to come finally reaching them. Lark waited, The Shepherd waited. The mounted bodyguard loosened a coil of of rope at his saddle and began to fashion a hangman's noose, one eye sardonically on Lark. The man Cory, seeing Lark's apparent resignation, let go of him. Art Rankine, on the other side, gave Lark's arm a quick squeeze before he let go.

Men came up the street now, spectators lagging behind them. Two Joshuans with Herb Racklin, the gunsmith. Two more with Jim Warner, the

176

harness maker. The four Joshuans all seemed to be cast from the same mold as Cory, hard-bitten, cold-eyed, no drop of mercy in them. They were taking a warped pleasure from their roles.

"Where are we going to do the deed, Shepherd?" one Joshuan asked, giving Warner an uncalled-for shove.

The Shepherd combed his beard thoughtfully with his fingers. He pointed. "See that new building? The rafters are up, and just high enough for our purpose. As soon as we bring in the women to watch . . ."

A man pushed purposefully through the ring of people, a small man with a badge on his vest. Stepping in front of Lark, Adam Beckett looked up at the Shepherd. "No man will be hanged without a fair trial in my jurisdiction, Danville. Moreover, you and your men have no standing in any court of law. You are criminals. I have witnesses and evidence that you are all guilty in New Eden of a federal offense, namely, polygamy."

Beckett stepped back and waved a hand to the sheriff. "Sheriff Slagg, do your duty, arrest this man, and these others. Lock them in your jail until they can make bail. I have filed a federal information against them."

Slagg stared at Beckett in disbelief. He stammered, "Why, I cain't do that, Beckett. The Reverend Danville is a respected citizen of Hardup County. I cain't toss him into the calaboose like some common criminal."

"Then I'll arrest him myself," Beckett said

harshly. With his left hand he pulled a pair of handcuffs from a hip pocket. "Get off your horse, Danville. As an officer of the United States, I arrest you for aiding, abetting, and practicing the crime of polygamy, and remand you to the custody of Sheriff Slagg until court convenes to try you."

The little guy has guts, Lark thought, more guts than sense. What will Danville do?

The Shepherd laughed, a great uproarious laugh. His beard vibrated, his belted girth shaking. "Little man, would you pit yourself against the might and authority of The Shepherd? Tex, take that popgun away from him and snap his own shackles on him." He waved back the tense mastiffs of his bodyguard and drew his own revolver. The hammer clicked to full cock.

Beckett, Lark realized, in his conceit could not imagine that anyone would challenge the might of the U.S. government. Too late his hand swept toward the nickeled pistol in his belt. Startled, The Shepherd hesitated a moment before he fired. It was enough so that in the very instant that Adam Beckett was a dead man, he managed to fire. The little marshal crumpled into the dust. Danville grunted, dropped his revolver, and clasped both hands over his ample belly, sagging forward in the saddle.

Lark's pistol barrel slammed the man Cory alongside the head, and even as Cory fell, Lark shot the man Tex dead. Tex's shot sent window glass tinkling from a store front, then the man toppled from the saddle. His startled horse reared and plunged away, dragging the gunman whose foot had caught in a stirrup. Two of the spectators caught and gentled the horse.

From the hotel window a rifle slammed, and another of the Joshuans went down. Like the trump of Gabriel came Tetrault's voice, "Drop your guns, you Joshuans, or you're all dead men!" Four complied—one of them Art Rankine—but the last man flung a shot toward the window. The rifle spanged, and the impact of the .45-90 slug spun the Joshuan like a rag doll before the man plunged facedown into the dust of the street and lay forever motionless.

Lark, tiger-tense, saw that the situation was under control. He said softly from the side of his mouth, "Art, play the Joshuan. It'll get you back to New Eden." He saw Tetrault and Collins come running from the hotel, Marley Belote and Jubal Harnish step out of the crowd behind Racklin and Warner with drawn guns. He heard Danville groan, "I'm shot, boys. Get me a doctor, someone."

Lark called to Collins, "Come on, Bill, we've got to get to Kate's. Con, take care of this pigeon, and get a doctor—oh, here he comes now."

A spectator propelled an obviously drunk Dr. Kermit into the circle. He dropped on his knees beside Beckett, fumbled about, and looked up owlishly. He said, "'Sno use, man's dead already."

"It's The Shepherd that's shot, you goddam fool!" one of the crowd said. As Collins joined Lark, Lark saw the doctor look up at The Shepherd with dazed eyes. The black horse edged away nervously, and Lark heard Danville grunt, "Get away from me, you damned incompetent! I can die without your help." Men of the crowd reached up to lift The Shepherd from his horse.

Lark did not wait for more. He and Collins shouldered through the crowd and took off up the side street at a run. They turned the corner and raced toward Kate Muldoon's cottage. To Lark's relief, he saw Val Kleberg, Kate, and Diane standing on the front porch. Diane carried her rifle.

As he and Collins ran through the gate and up the path, Lark saw a body facedown in Kate's nasturtiums, another sprawled unmoving at the foot of the porch steps.

Diane thrust the rifle at Kleberg and dove into Lark's arms. "Oh, Justin, I k-k-killed a man!" she wailed.

He said, "It's all right, baby. Take it easy." Over her shoulder he asked Kleberg what happened.

"I guess these animals thought they didn't have a thing to fear from a lone woman," Kleberg said. "They came through the gate with guns drawn and one yelled 'Come out of there, you bitch!' He blew a couple shots through the window, and Diane and I let them have it. She blew half one of 'em's head off, and I got the other."

"Good work, they had it coming," Lark said. "They were planning to hang both girls." That was an exaggeration, but it would serve, for the fate planned for the two women would have been more horrible than hanging.

"What about the rest?" Kleberg asked.

"Pretty fair cleanup," Lark said, untangling

Diane's arms from his neck. As she grew calmer and dried her eyes, he added, "Marshall Beckett got himself killed, the damned fool. We downed the Joshuan Tex and another man for good, and one of 'em named Cory will have a sore head for a month. Before he died the marshal gut-shot Danville, and I think he's hurt pretty bad. They were starting to work on him when we left."

"Half the army, and the kingpin himself," Kleberg said with a note of satisfaction. "But there's still New Eden, and Elihu Noon, and the rest of the Joshuans."

"That's right. We managed to keep Art Rankine in the clear, though, we didn't blow his cover. I've got to get him back to New Eden."

"We'll figure out something," Kleberg said. "Girls, why don't you come with us over to the hotel, until we've sent the wagon around to remove this carrion?"

When they entered Main Street, the remnants of the crowd were still milling about. Lark found Sheriff Slagg and had him send a deputy to remove the two corpses from Kate's front lawn. The sheriff seemed pleased to have something official to do.

When the deputy was gone, Lark said, "Sheriff, you realize you are in a mighty tight bind. Uncle Sam isn't going to like it one bit to have one of his marshals shot to death in your town. You'd better get a wire off to Miles City with the whole story. Best for you if they hear it from you first. You might get off with five to ten in Leavenworth."

"Oh, my God, Lark, you think they'll try me?" Slagg cried.

"Not if you change sides and fast. Send the wire, putting your best foot forward. Lock up the four Joshuans that didn't get in the way of a slug, and keep them on ice. Get together with Toney and the county attorney and the others of your gang and get your stories to jibe. How's The Shepherd?"

Slagg shook his head. "Not good. Beckett's bullet took him in the gut. Doc's sobered up and is working on Danville. He don't think the man will make it."

"There may be hell to pay at New Eden," Lark said. "You know Elihu Noon?"

"Yeah, he's a religious fanatic. I s'pose he'll be in charge now."

"Which isn't good. But he won't move as long as The Shepherd is alive. So keep your fingers crossed, Slagg. You may have to ride out there with me."

The four Joshuans, one with a bloody bandage around his head, were standing on the hotel porch under the guns of Lark's men. "The sheriff is taking over, Jubal," Lark said. "These four reprobates will be spending a night in jail. And maybe the rest of their lives."

"We didn't do nothin', Mr. Lark," Art Rankine said. "We didn't shoot nobody, and we ain't got none of them wives."

"Well, good for you, Flaherty. You might get a break for that. But you'll have to go to jail anyhow for the time being." Lark told him. Rankine looked sadly at Lark as he turned away. I need him undercover, Lark thought, and a night in jail won't hurt him much, barring a louse and a bedbug or two. He'll get even sometime though, I'd bet my poke on it.

Inside the hotel, Lark learned The Shepherd had been taken into the Morris' apartment on the ground floor. Shank Morris was at the desk, looking harried. Lark asked, "How's Danville, Shank?"

The hotelman shook his head. "Doc doubts iff'n he'll make it until morning. Say, Mr. Lark, what's gonna happen with New Eden now?"

"Damned if I know, Shank. Probably Elihu Noon will carry on. Though only God knows who will be left after the law is through cleaning up this mess."

"I didn't have no part in it, Mr. Lark," Morris said quickly. "A feller hasta kinda go along with some things, iff'n he wants to stay in business. You know that."

"But you knew what was going on, Shank, you knew plenty. Say, there's a thing called turning state's evidence. Think about it."

Diane and Kate Muldoon were standing near the door of the Morris apartment. Kate said, "Mrs. Morris is helping Dr. Kermit. I'm going to volunteer, Justin. I'm a good practical nurse, and I must do what I can."

"After what the man has done to Hardup County? You're an angel, Kate. Here comes the doctor now."

Dr. Kermit, his lined face gray, came out of the apartment and closed the door behind him. He accepted Kate's offer. "Thanks, Miss Muldoon,

Mrs. Morris can use your help. You won't be needed long anyhow, I'm afraid. Only his tremendous vitality is keeping Danville going. If he sees the morning light I'll be surprised."

As Kate went inside, Diane saw Lark draw Dr. Kermit aside and the two went upstairs. To the doctor, Lark said, "I know you're all in, doctor, but I must ask a few questions. First what about Elihu Noon?"

"A crazy man, Lark, a real lunacy case. Steer clear of him."

"If I can. Beyond that, what are they using to drug the disciples at New Eden?"

"I don't know," Kermit said brusquely. "Some kind of opium or coca derivative, I suppose."

"But you did know about it? I thought so. Third and finally, what happens to the children of New Eden?"

The doctor's gray face turned paler. "Wh—why, nothing, Lark. There might be—ah, a high incidence of childhood deaths, but that's normal in a frontier community. Croup, you know, and measles and cholera."

"Not to the point of extinction, doctor. I'm afraid an inquiry may point a finger at you. Somebody has helped those babies out of this world."

"I had—I had nothing to do with it," Kermit mumbled.

"But you signed the death certificates," Lark said, taking a shot in the dark. "If I were you, I'd inspect my records, and I'd have a good story cooked up for the investigators when they get here.

This affair has broken wide open, doctor, and I wouldn't give a plugged nickel for the chances of staying out of jail for those deeply involved."

"Not me, I'm in the clear," Kermit said, but his voice was shaky. "Excuse me, Lark, I've got to go. Got to take some medicine."

They have a good supply at the Silver Dollar, Lark thought. He felt a bit sorry for the man, a weak man, a boozer, drawn into an easy money plot that looked so safe. Now the piper was waiting to be paid.

He went upstairs, knowing Diane wanted to cry on his shoulder.

## Chapter XIII

A pounding on the door of his room brought Lark up from a troubled sleep. He called out, "Who is it?"

"Sheriff Slagg. Lark, I gotta talk to you."

Lark glanced at his watch on the nightstand—five-thirty A.M. He struggled into trousers and shirt and opened the door. He asked sleepily, "What's up, sheriff?"

"There's hell to pay. I was on watch in the lobby, dozing kinda, when the Muldoon woman came out of Morris's rooms to tell me The Shepherd was dead. I went over to Doc's office to rout him out for a death certificate, and the son-of-a-bitch was dead, too. Killed himself with some kinda injection."

"Scared. Afraid of what the Joshuans would do to him. And they would have," Lark said. "Come in and sit, Sheriff. You look beat. You could use a stiff jolt. The bottle is on the dresser."

The sheriff poured a water tumbler of Lark's whiskey and gulped it down, the rim of the glass clicking against his false teeth. He poured another and holding it, sat down heavily in the rocker. Lark waited, sitting on the edge of the bed, awaiting eventualities, not greatly touched by Kermit's suicide.

"Just what brings you here, Slagg?" Lark asked.

The sheriff looked at him with bloodshot eyes. "Damned if I know what to do," he confessed. "Like you said, I'm up to my neck in this affair, and I want out. I figger my only chance is to get on the right side quick. Or to do the Dutch like Doc did. That I ain't about to do—m'wife would pray me into hell for sure."

"You're up the creek all right, Slagg. Tell you what, you side me and my men against the Joshuans from today on. You do and I'll see what I can do to wash you in the blood of the Lamb. You wired Miles City? Then we'll have government men in here by the end of the day. I'll talk to 'em."

"Them U.S. marshals won't get any more respect from the Joshuans that's left than I will," the sheriff said glumly. "Especially with Elihu Noon the new ramrod out to the colony. He's a crazy man, Lark, I mean, crazy."

"The more reason why we have to get those poor disciples out of the colony fast. God only knows what he'll try to do to them. A pitched battle, an open raid, is no good, too many would get hurt. We've got to find a way to keep Noon and his crowd busy until we can move safely. Suppose we try it this way . . ."

After the sheriff left at seven, Lark walked over to Kate Muldoon's house, more to see how she was than to expect breakfast, since Kate, as volunteer

187

nurse, had been up all night with Danville. He was surprised to find Diane Carvell preparing breakfast, with Kate, in dressing gown and slippers, sipping coffee at the table.

"I tried to sleep, but couldn't," Kate explained. "Justin, what a horrible twenty-four hours."

"It has been. You heard about Doc?"

"Yes, from Slagg. I suppose he couldn't face the consequences of Danville's death, nor the Joshuans, or worst, face himself."

"You're guessing Kermit was up to his fat chin in this business with babies? Well, so am I. Either he helped with that abomination, or he supplied the means," Lark said. "Maybe that's why he stayed drunk most of the time. He was haunted by the ghosts of slain children."

"How beastly!" Diane said. "Justin, with The Shepherd gone, what will we do? I'm worried sick about my people at New Eden." She set a plate of eggs, ham, and fried potatoes in front of Lark, and poured coffee.

Lark began to eat. He said, "We have a plan, and I've got the sheriff with us. It's one hell of a gamble, but here's what we've cooked up." When he finished outlining the proposal, he said, "Kate, you're a brave girl, but we've involved you in this far enough. You keep out of it tomorrow, and Diane can stay here with you."

"Oh no you don't, Mr. Justin Lark!" Diane cried. "It's my little family out in that crazy place. I must, must ride with you."

Lark surrendered. "All right. But you may be

dodging bullets."

"I did my part yesterday, didn't I?" she challenged. "I shot—I killed a man when I had to."

Lark finished eating, had another cup of coffee, and stood up. Kate was sound asleep in her chair. He dropped his napkin on the table. He said, "You're a good cook, kid. All right, you can go. But for today, stick around here with Kate. Don't go gallivanting off anywhere. I'll see you later."

Later, at the courthouse, Lark recognized among the horses tied at the hitch rail Danville's magnificent black. A farm wagon was coming from the wagon yard. It stopped in front of the building. Lark looked in the high-sided bed and saw a coffin of rough pine, and four long bundles wrapped in canvas. The driver tied the reins of the team to the brake handle and jumped down, as if hurrying away from his grisly cargo.

Sheriff Slagg, and his deputies with drawn pistols, brought four men out to the wagon. Cory, the man Lark had slugged, wore a stained bandage around his head. A second man had one arm in a sling and appeared in pain. One of the deputies had to help the two up onto the wagon seat.

To the remaining two, Sheriff Slagg said curtly, "All right, you Flaherty, you and Shorty get on your horses. Cory can drive the team, and I don't give a damn what Pasco does. I ain't sending anybody along with you to New Eden because you ain't got any place else to go, unless you want to get hung. Remember, if there's any hurt done to them disciples, you'll all answer for it. You pass that word to Noon."

Art Rankine, alias Flaherty, and Shorty, the other man, swung up into their saddles. Shorty asked something about their guns. Slagg guffawed. "If you're around next week, you can ask for 'em pretty please. Now get going, you got a long road west. Cory, better keep that team moving. I dunno how long your manifest will keep."

Cory, his face twisted, clucked to the team to set it in motion. The black horse, silver-mounted saddle empty, was tied at the rear of the wagon. As Rankine and Shorty rode past Lark, Rankine snarled, "I'll get you for this, Lark, and don't you forget it. This crummy jail . . ."

Lark laughed, genuinely amused. "Flaherty, you'd better count yourself lucky that you're not riding in the back with your pals. Don't threaten me, mister. We're likely to meet again tomorrow."

Standing beside the sheriff, Lark watched the little cavalcade as it turned toward the street that led to the New Eden road. How the mighty have fallen, he thought, remembering the arrogance of the corps of riders which had accompanied The Shepherd on earlier visits to Acheron.

Sheriff Slagg, too, was humbler. He looked drained, curiously deflated. He asked, "You think we're doing the right thing, Lark? We're handing four tough men back to Elihu Noon."

Lark didn't think it judicious to tell the sheriff that one of the riders was a Pinkerton man. "Two of them aren't good for much," he commented. "And any action has its element of risk, Sheriff. Even walking down Main Street in broad daylight. The way I figure it, Noon is busy as all hell with taking over as Shepherd. Tomorrow he'll be tied up with the funerals, he'll make a big thing of that. All of which gives us time to get organized to move in on him and the colony tomorrow."

Slagg frowned, his manner doubtful. "Well," he said in shoddy bravado, "the thing's your pigeon. Anything goes wrong, anybody gets killed, it's on your head, Lark, not mine." He turned to his two deputies. "You remember what I just said, boys. Lark's running the show, not me."

Lark said, "That's right as rain, Sheriff. I won't contradict you and your men when you testify before the grand jury."

Lark met the westbound as it pulled into the station. Only one lawman got off. Lark met him with a bear hug and a shout of "Scotty! You old reprobate, you're a sight for sore eyes."

Scotty Drake grinned and linked an arm with Lark. He was a solid, grizzled man, not young, with the air of authority. He and Lark knew and liked each other, having worked together on several difficult cases. Lark picked up Drake's suitcase and they walked toward the hotel.

"So Beckett got himself killed," Drake said.

"Yes, though he shot the man who killed him," Lark said. "Hiram Danville, called 'The Shepherd.' Died early this morning. Scotty, that marshal of yours had more guts than sense. He

191

tried to arrest the big boy right in the middle of Danville's hardcase gang."

"Beckett read too many dime novels," Drake said drily. "Seems he got his job because he was a nephew or some such of an Ohio congressman. The appointment went to his head pretty bad. I'll bet he's up there somewheres wondering why this Danville didn't shake in his boots when Beckett pulled his little nickel-plated gun. Ain't hard to get yourself killed in this line of work, Justin. So what are we up against here?"

In his room in the Morris House, Lark gave the marshal a resume of all that had happened, and the present situation. He told Drake what he and the sheriff had set up.

"Sounds like a plan that might work," Drake said. "Seems to me the whole deal turns on this man Noon, who is taking over as Shepherd."

"Right, and they say he's as crazy as a locoed cayuse. Or is he crazy like a fox? Scotty, there's a lot at stake in this New Eden deal—twenty thousand acres of land, good buildings, irrigated fields, valuable livestock. And I have a hunch there's plenty of cash stashed away in banks in New Eden accounts. Danville turned this sect into a one-man show, so now Noon will have it all right under his thumb. What he intends for it—"

"Well, we'll learn tomorrow," Drake said cheerfully. "You get your posse organized this afternoon, all good men, and I'll swear 'em in as deputy U.S. marshals. We should hit the colony early tomorrow, while they are busy planting the old Shepherd and his escort to Nirvana, or hell, whichever. We work it right, nobody will get hurt but them who deserve it."

"Even after the gang is busted, it will be a mess to sort out what's what and who's who," Lark said. "The word we get from Rankine and Sonya on the inside is that the poor disciples are kept docile with drugs of some kind."

As the posse gathered that afternoon, Lark observed cynically how many Acheron people had, they claimed, been against the Joshuans all the time. They would ride now, anxious to prove they were on the side of the law. Most of these Lark and Drake turned down. They took Herb Racklin and Jim Warner, and only two or three other locals. Still, with the sheriff and the Pinkerton men, quite an army was assembled. The word was passed—meet at the courthouse at six in the morning, armed and ready to ride.

It was after supper and the light was fading before all the chores were done. Lark was standing with Scotty Drake on the widewalk in front of the hotel, worrying about tomorrow's weather, which didn't look good. There were more people out and about at this hour than Lark had seen since coming to Acheron. The two men turned at the sound of a horse racing down the street toward them. Lark recognized Danville's great black horse, and the rider, Danny Henty.

The boy yanked the horse to a halt in front of them so abruptly a cloud of yellow dust spun up. He leaped from the saddle and ran toward Lark.

The black horse shuddered, coughed, and went to its knees. The noble head dropped, and horse rolled onto its side and lay unmoving.

"Mr. Lark, the Countess sent you this. She told me to hurry as if the devil was after me, so I did." Danny gave Lark a folded note.

Taking the note, Lark glanced at the crowd gathering around the downed horse. Dead, Lark was sure, and Diane's words came back to him, "Out of the Excelsior line, aneurism of the arteries, wouldn't own one of 'em." Poor beast—but how had Danny come to be riding him?

For privacy, Lark led Drake and the boy into the lobby of the Morris House. Beneath a lighted lamp he unfolded the note:

Justin darling:

When Art Rankine and the others arrived with the bodies in late afternoon, Noon went into a frenzy, swearing terrible vengeance. He said the U.S. government was subject to a higher power—his power. I think—I feel, the man plans something horrible. We all must go tomorrow to the New Eden cemetery on Mt. Moriah, for the mass funeral. Strike quickly and hard, for there is death in the air. Do not look for help from the disciples, they have been drugged until they are like sheep under the spell of The Shepherd. Art and I will do what we can, but hurry.

I love you,
Your Sonya

Lark gave the note to Drake. He asked Danny, "How did the Countess reach you? Where did you get the horse?"

"A cowboy ridin' by told us about the shootout yestiddy, so I wanted to see what was cookin' at New Eden. I went in like always. Von was lookin' for me. He said there wa'nt no guards on duty, everyone in the place was shook up. He said the new Shepherd was wild, and he was scairt for himself and his sisters. We talked a long time. Then a rider come on a black horse and I ducked, but it was the Countess. She gave me the note and told me to ride 'like ze vind.' she said. I jumped on the black and the last I saw of the Countess and Von they was walkin' toward the community hall. Gosh, your wife is pretty, Mr. Lark."

"She is that indeed, Danny," Lark said. "You did right well, son. But you can't go back to Circle H tonight. I don't want you pirooting around in the dark the way things are. You go over to Kate Muldoon's for the night, and in the morning we'll find you a mount and you can ride."

"Gramma will be worried sick," Danny said, frowning.

"I know, but it can't be helped," Lark said. "Now scoot."

When the boy was gone, Drake gave the note back to Lark. "I don't like the sound of this," he said. "It looks like hell to pay. Don't you think we'd better pass the word to the posse that we're riding at five, not six? It will be light enough, and we've got a three-hour ride, even if we push the horses."

"You're right. I'll have Val Kleberg and Bill Collins pass the word to every man who is riding," Lark said. The thought of Sonya in danger brought a hollow feeling in the pit of his stomach.

It was a tough and competent little army that gathered in the dawn light at the Hardup County courthouse. Lark was dismayed to see Diane Carvell among them, in riding habit, with her .45-90 tucked in the saddle boot. So was Danny Henty, on a foxy little pony he had borrowed from Kate, though the boy was unarmed. Lark scowled, but there was no time for argument. He looked at Scotty Drake, who nodded, and Lark stood in his stirrups. He brought his arm up and forward, and the riders shook their horses into a trot toward the New Eden road. A cheer went up from a small group of bystanders.

They rode fast, but not at a pace that taxed the horses. Lark dropped back to ride with Danny and Diane, for Sonya had not given the location of Mt. Moriah. He asked Danny, but the boy did not know for sure. He thought it was on a high hilltop some distance west of the colony, toward the high peaks. A thought chilled Lark—sounds like a place Noon could fort up, and be damned hard to get at.

"Our sheriff doesn't look happy," Scotty said, dropping back.

"It has dawned on Slagg that he doesn't have a Chinaman's chance of dodging a grand jury indictment," Lark said. "He has been eating out of the trough too long. He'd rather be any place but here, but it's the only way he can salvage any good will."

"He's sure to be kicked out of his sheriff's job, and likely he'll go to the pen besides," Drake said. "He'll try to call it legitimate graft, but it won't work. Goddamn it, Justin, the one thing I can't stand without puking is a crooked lawman."

They came to the gate in the four-wire fence that went clear around the New Eden land. It was locked and double-locked. Con Tetrault slid down from his horse and severed the strands with a pair of wire cutters. The riders trotted through and set a fast pace toward New Eden.

When the buildings of the colony came in sight, Lark sent two scouts ahead. When they returned to the main group, Jubal Harnish reported, "Not a soul in sight. Everything looks peaceful."

"If they ain't gone, they're layin' awful quiet waitin' for us," Marley Belote added.

Lark stood in his stirrups to stare at the buildings of the colony with Bill Collins's field glasses. In the fields cattle grazed, in a pasture a few horses stood contentedly, switching tails. Through the garden fields water gleamed in the irrigation ditches. A setting of pastoral peace, Lark thought, but it might be a deadly trap. Yet there were lives at stake. He had to chance it.

"Let's move in, boys," he called. "Spread out. No shooting, mind you, unless you're directly fired upon."

Fanning out in a wide arc, guns ready, the riders swept toward the buildings. Lark took Diane and Danny Henty under his figurative wing, riding in. He felt a cold spot between his shoulder blades as they neared the silent colony. Still no shots sounded, still no man nor woman appeared. The riders reached the barns and sheds in an eerie silence that was ominous of something monstrous waiting. The place seems just like Oliver Goldsmith's *Deserted Village*, Lark thought.

"Search all buildings!" Lark called to his men. He swung down from his horse. He saw Diane slide her rifle from the saddle boot and hand it to Danny. Immodestly, she raised her skirt and drew a small pistol from a holster strapped to her leg. A regular amazon, Lark thought, and grinned as she said, "Lead on, Justin. We're ready for war."

Warily, the three entered a long barn. The cows had been turned out, but the sultry air was heavy with the cloying sweet smell of cattle and the sharp ammonia smell of manure. The main floor was empty. Motioning Diane and the boy to cover him, Lark drew his pistol and climbed the ladder to the loft. Nothing.

They hurried through the building and out the far door. Next was a large horse barn, its only occupants a mare with her new colt. She eyed them suspiciously, but the colt paid no attention, too busy on shaky splayed legs trying to get his lunch from his mother.

Again Lark climbed the loft ladder. But as his head lifted through the opening, a voice cried harshly, "Don't you come no farther or I'll put a slug through you!" The muzzle of a rifle looked Lark right in the eye.

Danny Henty recognized the voice. "Hey, that's gramma! Gramma, don't shoot, it's Mister Lark and Miss Carvell and me."

"Oh, thank the good God!" Mrs. Henty said. "Come on up."

Lark holstered his pistol and climbed into the loft. Diane and the boy followed. Beyond Mrs. Henty, Lark saw a figure bedded under a blanket in the loose hay. It moaned softly.

"My daughter-in-law, Ruby," Mrs. Henty said, her voice thick with emotion. "Danny's ma. Look what them devils done to her."

In the gray light from a high window, they saw that the woman had been beaten to a pulp. Lark and Diane knelt beside her. Danny, sobbing, held his mother's hand. Her face was a massive bruise, purple and green and yellow, the skin scarified. She stared at them through slitted swollen eyes, her breathing stertorous.

"When Danny didn't come home, at first light I loaded the Spencer," Mrs. Henty explained. "One time he showed me where the secret trail started, so I went on up it. Got to the dam, seen nobody around, so I got bold. Found Ruby in one of the cottages, barely able to walk. I was skeered they might come back and kill both of us, so I got her across the yard and up here. I figgered I could at least give 'em a fight from up here." What a superhuman effort the spare old woman must

199

have needed to get Ruby up the ladder Lark thought. Diane smoothed the tangled hair back from the woman's once pretty face.

Lark leaned down. "Ruby, can you understand me? Where have they all gone, the Joshuans, the disciples, and Elihu Noon?"

"To Mt. Moriah, to the cemetery," she whispered. "That terrible place where they bury the old folks and the dead new babies. Noon is raving. He says we are all going to the ultimate Eden. He says we will offer sacrifice, like Abraham offered Isaac. That will take us, Noon says to a new land, a land of milk and honey where there is no hunger, no pain. Where there is no death forever, but for the just there is only love, love, love." Ruby's eyes closed as if the effort had exhausted her.

Danny touched Ruby's bruised cheek. "Oh, mama, who did this to you?" he wailed.

"Monte Marshall's replacement," she said, rage strengthening her voice. "A man called Cory. Finally the new Shepherd himself because I couldn't walk with the rest to Mt. Moriah. He said I could stay behind and be damned forever."

"You're lucky," Lark said grimly, and stood up. "Danny, you stay here with your mother and gramma. We'll send help as soon as we can. We've got to go now. I think you'll be safe enough."

"We'll take care of ourselves," Mrs. Henty said. "Just you get every one of them murderin' devils, especially that terrible man Noon. You hear me, Justin Lark?" Her voice was fierce.

At the foot of the ladder Diane slid up her

200

divided skirt and replaced the little pistol. She picked up her rifle Danny had dropped. Lark, regretting the delay, ran with her across the yard to the cow barn, and through it to their horses. He saw that the dark clouds to the west were heavier. The air was sultry, only now and then a vagrant breeze disturbing the dust of the yard. Now a few big drops of rain spattered on the roofs, and he heard a distant rumble of thunder.

Mounting, Lark and Diane rode toward the community hall where they could see the others gathered. Val Kleberg rode to meet them. He said, "Not a soul here, Justin. Well, almost—we found Cory and Pasco. Dead, shot in the head from behind. Looks as if The Shepherd doesn't have any mercy for crippled sheep."

"Or herders," Lark said. Quickly he told of finding the Hentys. "Glad they're out of it, and the boy," he added.

"Damned tootin', things are getting thick," Scotty Drake said, frowning. "We'd better get to that Mt. Moriah in one hell of a hurry. How far is it?"

Lark jerked a thumb at Sheriff Slagg. "How far, Sheriff?"

"I was only there onst, but I'd guess about five miles," Slagg said. "The last part to the top is hellish steep. The top is mostly flat, rocky, about three-four acres. Big graveyard with white markers. Guess they'll be halfway there when the last trump sounds." Slagg chuckled at his poor witticism. Drake scowled at him.

"I'm getting more and more afraid of what that maniac intends to do," Lark said. "Let's ride, boys."

## Chapter XIV

There was no mistaking the road to Mt. Moriah. The twin ruts of wagon wheels, the tracks of steel-shod hoofs, the impressions of human feet. As the posse rode farther, there were other signs—a torn piece of stained cloth, drops of new blood on a wide leaf. Lark swore softly. Elihu Noon, the new Shepherd, was forcing these poor souls over rock and thorn on a veritable Via Crucis. At the end of it did death await, even as it had for the Christ? Noon must be stopped.

The riders splashed through the icy waters of a small mountain creek. In the spray of silver droplets, Lark had the vagrant thought of how comforting this cold water must have been for those tortured bare feet, even though the respite was fleeting.

Con Tetrault came up to ride between Lark and Diane. "You didn't know, Justin, you were in the barns, but we found some of the damndest things. Danville's cottage is a regular mansion, with oil paintings and art work, and Persian rugs and stuff. He had a grand piano, and closets full of costumes.

There are silk sheets on the beds, the shelves are filled with books. And you've got to believe me, there's a harp there, a big one, all gold."

"He won't need it where he's gone," Diane said sharply. "Maybe the devil will send him back for it."

"Maybe. Then when we were leaving, Val smelled something and we checked. There was coal oil poured over the bottom boards outside. It had been set afire and charred some places, but the fire went out."

"The new Shepherd wanted to cancel the worldliness of the old one, and destroy all his carnal possessions," Lark guessed.

"Could be," Tetrault said. "Sure was a contrast to Noon's diggings. I never saw a monk's cell, but Noon's cottage must be like one. Hardly any furniture, few clothes, mostly dark robes. The pictures on his wall were those dark and doleful ones—Durer prints and the like. Hanging on the wall was a length of thin chain, and it was clotted with blood. His own, I guess."

"A man who endures self-flagellation for his sins wouldn't be tempted by the riches of New Eden," Lark said slowly. "This world's goods would mean nothing to him. I'm afraid, Con, of what that indicates."

Tetrault nodded, his face grave. "Noon doesn't intend to return from Mt. Moriah. And he will take every disciple and Joshuan with him on his last dark journey."

"Oh, God, Justin, he'll kill my sisters and my brother!" Diane cried. "Will he shoot them as he did Cory and Pasco, shoot them all, and then himself?"

"I can't guess," Lark said. "He must have some scheme all prepared. Something more sinister than gunfire, I would think."

"Poison!" she exclaimed.

"Could be. As for getting them to take it, remember most of the people are enslaved to drugs. Others like Lavon and the girls, who have avoided the habit, well—" He shrugged, feeling terror rising in him. He shook it off.

They circled the base of a hill and Mt. Moriah loomed ahead of them. It was hardly a mountain, more of a butte, a truncated cone rising sharply against a backdrop of snow-streaked peaks and menacing clouds. A crooked trail led in zigzags up its slope. The wagon was stopped at the foot of the trail, for it would be negotiable only by horsemen and people on foot—people like white-robed pilgrims with bleeding feet.

The pilgrims were climbing. Lark could see them in their white robes, distinct against the greens and tans of the mountain foliage. At the head of the antlike procession a group of figures struggled under the burden of the wooden coffin, while behind them others were bent low beneath the cumbersome packs that were the wrapped corpses. What irony it is, Lark thought, that these poor acolytes will never, never return by this road, if Noon has his way. I am certain of that now, and it must be stopped.

He borrowed the field glasses again from Collins. Through the lenses the figures were brought close, even to recognition. With a lift of the heart he saw Art Rankine, and Rankine was armed. And below him, in the toiling mass of the acolytes, he saw a woman with the hood of her robe thrown back, his wife Sonya, still alive, still safe, thank God.

Leading the procession, almost to the flat of the butte's top, Lark saw a figure in red. Elihu Noon. Against the crimson of the robe, Lark could see the gold-inlaid staff glint in the dull light. Noon was the epitome of the Old Testament prophet, hair and beard blowing wildly in the stiff wind, exhorting his followers for more speed. Down the line a black-clad Joshuan swung a quirt against the back of a disciple who had staggered under his load.

Now a Joshuan brought up a little pack mule, pushing some of the pilgrims aside. There were two small casks lashed to the pack saddle. Powder kegs? Lark wondered. If they were, and Noon set them both off at once, there was enough explosive to tear the top off the mountain, and every living soul with it!

Handing the glasses back to Collins, he said to Scotty Drake, "They'll soon reach the top. We've got to move fast or someone will get hurt. Any chance, Scotty, we could circle around and come at them from both sides?"

"It's worth a try," the marshal said. "Notice how misty it's getting? Might give us some cover. I'll take one column, you take the other."

Lark gave terse orders. Scotty and his group broke away from the main trail and rode into a coulee leading to the right. Lark said to Slagg, "Sheriff, you and your men ride over to the bottom of the main trail and hold. Don't do any shooting unless a Joshuan takes a crack at you." Without waiting for answer or objection, Lark wheeled his horse and with his men rode toward the base of the butte.

A hundred yards along, a dry wash cut down the hillside to the creek which tumbled along the coulee. Scotty Drake and his men had gone on along the creek, hoping to circle behind the mountain, but Lark stopped here and dismounted. He said, "It's Shank's mare from here, boys. This wash will give us some cover, I think it runs almost to the top." He looked over his crew—Diane Carvell, Tetrault and Kleberg, and Herb Racklin, the gunsmith, chosen for his skill with a rifle. "Keep your heads down. Let's go," he said.

The steep wash was dry now, but if the clouds above let go it could become a raging torrent. The mist was cool on his face as Lark climbed, and the grumble of thunder had become heavy. The flashes of lightning were vicious now, hurting the eyeballs, temporarily blinding.

Lark had taken the last position among the climbers. Just ahead of him, Diane slipped on rough stones and loose clay. She must have barked some knuckles, for she swore softly and licked the damaged fingers. Then she went on climbing. Good girl, Lark thought. She's sick with worry about her family up there, but she keeps going. And so must I, though if anything happens to Sonya, whoever does it will pay and pay and pay.

Wind gusted now, a storm front flattening the sparse grass and whipping the thin underbrush along the edges of the wash. It grew steeper, and they climbed right into the teeth of the storm. A chunk of rock came tumbling down, and Lark lurched to safety as it spun past him.

Finding a narrow ledge, he stood up to check their progress. That was a mistake, for from his left a rifle spanged, and a slug *skreed* off into the distance, inches from his head. He jumped back into the wash, keeping low.

The climbers were lucky. Where the crevasse thinned and flattened near the top, twisted juniper and buckbrush and stunted jackpine had eked out a foothold. Lark gained this copse and lay flat like the others. He saw that Diane's skirt was ripped from hip to hem, revealing white flesh, but she paid no attention. As she turned to Lark he saw that blood had seeped from a narrow gouge on her forehead. But she clung to her rifle, her face cold and determined. She looked a question at Lark, but he shook his head.

Val Kleberg slid back from under a juniper just at the rim. He said, "The Shepherd is trying to keep order and hurry the pallbearers, and they're dam' near bushed, the poor bastards. The crowd will soon be gathered. All as soaked as drowned rats."

"As we are," Lark said. Pouring rain made the duff of the thicket and the raw clay and the scanty grass wet and treacherous for footing. He made a brace on a boulder. He said, "Any sign of—" but a crash of thunder drowned his words. When it subsided he asked, "Any sign of Scotty and his men?"

"Not yet," Kleberg said.

"Let's find places along the rim where we can observe, while we wait for Scotty," Lark said. "And for God's sake, keep your heads down."

While the three others fanned out, Lark took Diane Carvell straight ahead up the almost precipitous slope. They found a place of conceal-ment, though the hiding place was no protection from the slash of the cold rain. Carefully they squirmed up until they could see across the flat.

The casket was, Lark saw, placed on the west side of a great boulder, with the four wrapped corpses beside it. Now the last of the disciples stumbled over the rim and joined the others. The little mule with the casks, wanting no part of this, was literally dragged up the last pitch by two cursing Joshuans. The two black-clad men teth-ered the mule and joined a third, who was standing at one side. As the two men dismounted, Lark saw with relief that one of the three was Art Rankine, and he was still armed. One man held a rifle, and was gesticulating toward the slope be-low. I'm glad you weren't a better shot, mister, Lark thought solemnly.

He watched the throng of disciples gathered around The Shepherd. Sonya—Sonya—ah, there she was, beautiful in her shapeless white robes. With all his mind he willed her to move away, toward him, out of the crowd. Whether it was his telepathy, or because Sonya sensed some move-ment below the rim, he didn't know, but to his joy she broke out of the press around Noon.

Noon was resplendent though a little bedraggled by rain in his crimson robes, carrying the great golden shepherd's crook that was his symbol of authority. Now he mounted a ledge of rock facing the crowd below him. Beyond The Shepherd's pulpit Lark could see row on row of small white markers. My god, Lark thought, there are more people buried here than live in the town of Acheron.

Ignoring the rain, a big man in a white robe untied the casks from the pack mule and set them on rock at the feet of The Shepherd. The mule, freed of his burden, kicked up his heels and bolted past Rankine and Shorty, who let the mule tear headlong down the trail. Unperturbed, the disciple set the casks on their sides and blocked them into place with stones. Now another disciple brought a sack. He emptied dozens of tin cups from it. As the man ranged the cups beside the casks, Lark was relieved by the knowledge that the contents of the kegs was not powder. But what?

The rumble and crash of thunder was so loud and frequent Diane could speak to Lark without whispering. "Look at that man, Justin—as terrible as a prophet from the Old Testament! What will he do to these poor people? He's saying something, can you make it out?"

Masterful on his eminence, Noon was preaching hellfire and brimstone. The racket of the storm made hellish counterpoint to what he was saying, though at this distance Lark and Diane could catch only a word, a phrase, occasionally a sentence. Now The Shepherd raised his high-pitched voice louder to carry above the storm.

"Ye men of sin . . . of death . . . immoral, tainted . . . rotted by the sickness of the flesh . . . yet I will save ye, make ye whole, for I am The Shepherd . . . ye shall be washed clean if . . . drink deep of my Nepenthe . . . to enter my newer Eden . . . this earth, unfit for ye anointed . . . wicked men pursue us . . . before they come, drink . . . all ye who believe, drink my potion and be saved . . . I am with ye all days . . . take cups, fill . . . wait until all are ready . . . drink with me."

The red-robed figure, looking nine feet tall above the crowd, raised the golden crook in command. "Come, ye fearful ones! Believe and ye will see the ultimate Eden . . . ye of little faith . . . fill the cup and drink deep . . . ye will be with me . . ."

The stout disciple who had placed the kegs took a cup and filled it from the spigot on a cask. Raising the pannikin in salute to The Shepherd, he stepped back, holding the filled cup against his breast. A woman followed his lead, and behind her the other disciples formed a line in the driving rain. As cups were filled, the disciples waited for Noon's word.

"Justin, what is it?" Diane gasped. "Some kind of wine?"

"Wine of death," Lark said, the fearful truth of Noon's intentions apparent now. "They will drink and die, even The Shepherd. There's poison in those casks."

He clambered over the rim, careless of consequences. He raised his rifle. A forked white flash blinded him, a tremendous crash deafened him. In the gray light he saw four of the white-robed acolytes running toward him, their hands empty. He swung an arm toward them and they tumbled over the rim, Lavon Carvell, and two young women. The fourth flung herself into Lark's arms, sobbing. "Oh, Justin, zat terrible man! He has poison there, he will kill zem!"

"We'll stop him," Lark said grimly. "Slide down with the others and wait, darling."

He shouted, "Val—Con—Racklin—let's go! Hit the top!"

In the open, he saw that the last of the disciples were filling their cups. All were waiting the order from Noon—the order to drink and die. The Shepherd screamed "Are ye ready? Then come with me to the ultimate Eden!" He had one of the pannikins in his hand. He raised it high. In the other hand the golden shepherd's crook pointed to the sky. "Partake, partake of my blessed potion and ye will—"

A bolt of lightning struck with a terrible crash, shaking the mountain top. In the stunning impact, the crimson figure of Elihu Noon flared into unholy light, incandescent. In his hand the golden staff exploded. Dazzled and deafened, people fell to their knees, fell on their faces. In the moments following, the dimness seemed as impenetrable as smoke.

Lark found himself running toward the crowd. There was a smell of sulphur and ozone and charred cloth in the air. The stone where The Shepherd had stood was empty. Regardless of the danger, Lark sprang to the ledge. He fired three shots from his rifle into the air. He yelled, "Don't drink! Throw your cups away! It's deadly poison!"

The tremendous bolt which had struck Noon seemed to bring a culmination to the fury of the storm. The rain slowed, the sky began to lighten, though flares of electricity still ran forked and luminous along the peaks. In the dull light Lark saw that some of the people had spilled their cups, now others slowly tipped theirs and let the liquid fall to the ground. Only the man who had prepared the casks and drawn the first cupful stood defiant. He raised his pannikin to his lips and drank. He stood motionless for a long moment. Then he screamed and dropped the cup. Retching, he clasped his hands to his middle. He sagged forward, then slumped to the ground, not even stretching out his hands to break his fall. He lay so flaccid and unmoving Lark was sure the man was dead before he hit the ground.

The rest of Lark's people came over the rim. From the far side, racing through the cemetery, came Scotty Drake and his party. They moved through the crowd, striking any remaining cups from nerveless hands. Lark looked anxiously toward the head of the trail, then grinned when he saw that Art Rankine had the two Joshuans under his gun.

Val Kleberg and Con Tetrault each seized one of the casks and hurled them over the cliff to smash in a clatter of burst staves on the rocks below. Every tin cup was gathered, flattened, and buried in a deep crevice in the rock.

Lark found Rankine with his two prisoners. "Good work, Art. The sheriff and his men will be up soon, you can turn Shorty and his pal over to them. No trouble?"

"Nope, except I was afraid you wouldn't get here in time to keep some of the poor souls from drinking that hell brew. Well, when I kept the boys from drawing a bead on you, I guess I paid you for that night in Slagg's jail."

"Heaping coals of fire on my head, eh? Art, you're a true pal," Lark said, "What was in those casks?"

"Cyanide," the man Shorty said. "Noon stole it from the Gold Creek Mill. A guy named Pomeroy, once a chemist, fixed the mixture for Noon. I think The Shepherd scragged him then. I ain't seen Pomeroy around."

"Weren't you Joshuans supposed to drink, too?" Lark asked.

The man stared at him. "What kind of a dam' fool do you think I am? I hired out to Danville as a gunslinger, not to commit suicide."

"Good thinking," Lark said, grinning, and walked away.

He found Sonya and the Carvells trying to encourage the dispirited pilgrims, who were wet and cold and in a kind of shock. He said, "Good work, honey. Do what you can. I'm going to see what happened to Noon."

The body in the crimson robes behind the rocks

was curiously flat and shapeless. The great shock of hair was scorched away. The robes were slashed down the front clear to the flesh as if cut with a knife. The hand which had held the gold-inlaid croock was a charred ruin, and the staff itself was splintered. Disliking the task, Lark knelt and unbuckled a heavy money belt. He handed it to Scotty Drake.

"Noon won't need this in his ultimate Eden," Lark said. "It's part of the puzzle your office will have to take over, Scotty. New Eden has a slew of assets, but it will be a tangle to liquidate."

"I hope Danville kept books," Drake said. "I'm sure the courts will try to return what they can to the disciples as individuals. You think Noon intended to die with his flock?"

Lark shrugged. "He had the cup in his hand. I guess we'll never know."

Sheriff Slagg, very official, took over the few remaining Joshuans and had them led away. He was bent on taking Art Rankine too, until Lark intervened. "He's one of my men, not a Joshuan, Sheriff," Lark said.

"He's a hell of a good actor, then," the sheriff said grudgingly.

"I am, and my name isn't Flaherty, either," Rankine said, grinning. "But we'll let your records stand that way. By the way, you feed well in your jail. Tell Mrs. Slagg my compliments to her cooking."

As the sheriff left, Sonya and the Carvells gathered around Lark. Sonya said "Eet is true, Justin, ze babies, ze little ones, zey were killed. The headboards—two days old, a month, two months, row on row. What horrible beasts, to slaughter ze innocents in ze name of religion!"

Seeing how perturbed and saddened his wife was, Lark said gently, "It has happened before, honey, through the ages," and changed the subject. "Thank God the cleanup and caring for the poor souls is up to Scotty Drake and the U.S. Government," he said. "Diane, when we get you and Lavon and the girls back to Denver, the Pinkertons will be through. But we'll stick with the case until you have reclaimed what you can out of the New Eden assets."

"The work of the agency was marvelous, Justin," Diane said. "When the disciples lifted their cups of poison, I was relieved to know my three were empty-handed, and not stupid with drugs."

"We were for a while, Mr. Lark," Gracia Carvell said. "Oh, it was awful. My head felt as if it were stuffed with cotton wool. I did whatever I was told because I had no will of my own. Then Von caught on and warned us. When we avoided the food they drugged, they knew it. They didn't force drugs on us, but they made sure Kris and I didn't have a chance to run away. The Shepherd, Danville, he was going to m-m-marry us! That nasty old goat with his six wives. I'm glad he's dead."

"The drugs explain how the Shepherds could keep the people under control," Lark said. "And have them sign over their fortunes. Well, you're all well out of it with no damage except to your pride and your conscience."

"People died because of us, I think," Kris Carvell said slowly. "Mr. Lark, the Carvells will never be the same again. This has changed us."

"It has changed me, I tell you," Lavon said. "My stupidity—if I hadn't been such a jackass as to fall for Danville's pitch, none of the Carvells would have been mixed up with New Eden. I'm through with theology. I'm going to be a mining engineer."

"A smart choice," Lark said. "Now let's get away from this charnel house and return to civilization."

"If you can count Acheron in that category," Diane said tersely.

## Chapter XV

The clackety-clack of iron wheels over rail joints told Lark the train was making good time. Beside him Sonya dozed on the plush of the seat, her red lips moving softly as she breathed. He looked at her fondly, pleased at how beautiful his wife was, how brave, how dear to his heart. He smiled, remembering their last two nights in Acheron while the authorities wound up the details of the New Eden affair. Lark and Sonya, separated so long, threatened by the Shepherds, had found their ardor aroused, their love as passionate as it had been when they were first married three years before.

As the train chugged south through the Beaverhead toward the Idaho line, Lark could still not throw off the horrors of New Eden. He doubted if he ever could. Some good had come of the case. New Eden had been eradicated, the disciples had been freed from bondage. And the authorities had been awakened to the consequences of unbridled power. They had at last cleaned out the pigsty of Hardup County.

Some questions would never be answered, some dark deeds never explained. Some of the missing would never be found, though the headless body of the Siskiyou Kid had been resurrected and reinterred without suspicion of Lavon Carvell. The source of New Eden funds would always end in mystery, and what hand had slain the babies? Lark shook his head.

The New Eden property would come up for sale, and Lark had jokingly suggested to Diane that it fitted the original imaginary ranch they had used as a screen. Maybe she would like to bid it in.

The girl had been horrified. "Justin, a place haunted by the ghosts of dead people, by the wraiths of murdered babies! I would wake screaming at the terrible figure of Elihu Noon in his red robes calling the lightning down on himself. My darlings are safe. I never want to see Acheron again."

He had laughed and patted her hand. "All right, all right, I was only kidding. But there won't be any kidding when you get your Pinkerton bill from Sam Eames. It will rattle your slats."

"The cost I'll pay, and pay gladly," she said seriously. "But I'll never be able to pay the debt I owe you and your heroic men." She was silent for a while, then she brightened and said, "Justin, when you do forward my bill, have that Bill Collins of yours bring it by hand. I'd like to meet that handsome young man again."

"Bill won't mind that a bit," Lark said, laughing. "I'll see that Sam Eames provides the messenger service."

He looked over his shoulder now, to the end of the Pullman Palace car where the four Carvells sat, a family rejoined and happy. That's one of the rewards of my kind of work, he thought. To reunite families, to clear the innocent, to bring the guilty to justice. A large order—sometimes dangerous, sometimes dirty, sometimes unpalatable, but all to the weight in the scales of justice.

He wondered if he had been right in handling this case. So many had died, so many had been ruined. He had killed a man, been responsible for the deaths of several others. He did not like that, though it had been necessary. He had handled the affair in the time-tested tradition of Allan Pinkerton—scout, question, find informers, infiltrate, make your case with all the evidence, and then joined by the law, close in and end it.

Even success had brought a recurring worry. Was he growing to like too much the danger, the excitement, the sense of power he felt over the crook and the criminal? Was he losing his sense of proportion and seeing the whole world in terms of black and white, with no gray areas? Or should he let the agency do the worrying about the rights and the wrongs?

Sonya muttered softly in her sleep. He took her hand in his. There's my answer, he thought. This woman of mine has a strength and courage beyond my own. If I become harsh and unfeeling, she'll let me know, and she won't pull her punches. Tomorrow, with our baby son, she'll be all woman, all mother. Yet Sonya Verloff Lark is my mentor and my conscience. When in the hotel I told her something of my worries, she said, "You did your job, Justin Lark. Not perfectly, but you did it. You're my man."

Comforted, weariness overtook him, and he sagged into the red plush of the car seat, with the hand of his beautiful wife still in his. He closed his eyes, letting his body sway to the rhythm of the speeding train.

On the edge of sleep, a vagrant thought flitted through his mind—I wonder what Sam Eames is cooking up for the two of us when we get home.

# GREAT WESTERNS
## by Dan Parkinson

**THE SLANTED COLT**                     (1413, $2.25)

A tall, mysterious stranger named Kichener gave young Benjamin Franklin Blake a gift. It was a gun, a colt pistol, that had belonged to Ben's father. And when a cold-blooded killer vowed to put Ben six feet under, it was a sure thing that Ben would have to learn to use that gun — or die!

**GUNPOWDER GLORY**                     (1448, $2.50)

Jeremy Burke, breaking a deathbed promise to his pa, killed the lowdown Sutton boy who was the cause of his pa's death. But when the bullets started flying, he found there was more at stake than his own life as innocent people were caught in the crossfire of *Gunpowder Glory*.

**BLOOD ARROW**                     (1549, $2.50)

Randall Kerry returned to his camp to find his companion slaughtered and scalped. With a war cry as wild as the savages', the young scout raced forward with his pistol held high to meet them in battle.

**BROTHER WOLF**                     (1728, $2.95)

Only two men could help Lattimer run down the sheriff's killers — a stranger named Stillwell and an Apache who was as deadly with a Colt as he was with a knife. One of them would see justice done — from the muzzle of a six-gun.

**CALAMITY TRAIL**                     (1663, $2.95)

Charles Henry Clayton fled to the west to make his fortune, get married and settle down to a peaceful life. But the situation demanded that he strap on a six-gun and ride toward a showdown of gunpowder and blood that would send him galloping off to either death or glory on the . . . *Calamity Trail*.

*Available wherever paperbacks are sold, or order direct from the Publisher. Send cover price plus 50¢ per copy for mailing and handling to Zebra Books, Dept. 1903, 475 Park Avenue South, New York, N.Y. 10016. Residents of New York, New Jersey and Pennsylvania must include sales tax. DO NOT SEND CASH.*

## SAIGON COMMANDOS
### by Jonathan Cain

It is Vietnam as we've never seen it before, revealed with bitter reality and love — of a people and a place.

*Available wherever paperbacks are sold, or order direct from the Publisher. Send cover price plus 50¢ per copy for mailing and handling to Zebra Books, Dept. 1903, 475 Park Avenue South, New York, N.Y. 10016. Residents of New York, New Jersey and Pennsylvania must include sales tax. DO NOT SEND CASH.*